The Taming of a Tigress

STACKS

NEWARK PUBLIC LIBRARY

NEWARK, OHIO

G·K
Hall
&Co.

GAYLORD M

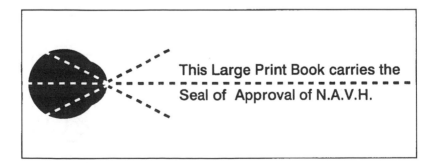

THE TAMING
OF A TIGRESS

Barbara Cartland

G.K. Hall & Co. • Thorndike, Maine

Published in 2001 by arrangement with International Book Marketing Limited.

G.K. Hall Large Print Paperback Series.

The text of this Large Print edition is unabridged.
Other aspects of the book may vary from the original edition.

Set in 16 pt. Plantin by Rick Gundberg.

Printed in the United States on permanent paper.

Library of Congress Cataloging-in-Publication Data

Cartland, Barbara, 1902–
    The taming of a tigress / Barbara Cartland.
        p.   cm.
    ISBN 0-7838-9401-5 (lg. print : sc : alk. paper)
    1. Kidnapping — Fiction. 2. England — Fiction. 3. Large type
books. I. Title.
PR6005.A765 T36 2001
    823´.912—dc21   00-069116

The Taming of a Tigress

author's note

As I have written in this novel, Astley started his Circus near Westminster Bridge.

Later it became an Amphitheatre with a stage, four tiers of boxes, and a Circus Ring in the centre.

It was the wonder of the world, and for nearly a century the most unusual and interesting displays and equestrian melodramas were produced there by its owner.

The jewels of India are fabulous, and many Maharajahs and Princes had their own private Mines.

The Maharajah of Hyderabad, reputedly the richest man in the world, had his own Diamond Mine, which I saw when I visited Hyderabad.

It is this Mine which produced the largest diamond in the world, the size of a hen's egg. Known as the Koh-i-Noor, it is now among the British Crown Jewels.

Next to Hyderabad the jewellery of the Maharajahs of Baroda are the most impressive. The Maharajah's stallion wears an emerald girdle.

A Maharajah of Kaparhala wore a clip of

three-thousand diamonds and pearls in his turban, while a Maharajah of Patiala was more spectacular.

He had five necklaces of diamonds and emeralds hung round his neck, he wore a belt of diamonds, and his scarf was held by a four-inch emerald.

The children of Their Highnesses played marbles with emeralds the size of panthers' eyes, and scattered pearls as if they were confetti.

One Indian Prince insisted that his wife should wear a Chastity Belt. She only agreed to this when it was made of diamonds!

chapter one

1826

"Do you mean you are refusing me?"

There was an incredulous note in the Duke of Wrexham's voice.

It was as if he could not believe such a thing was possible.

"I am sorry if it upsets you," Malvina Maulton replied, "but my answer is 'No!' "

The Duke stared at her. Then he said:

"Well, you have made a damned fool of me, there is no doubt about that!"

Malvina did not answer.

He walked away to stand at the window, looking out with unseeing eyes onto the garden.

"Every one of my friends was quite certain that you intended to accept me," he said, almost as if he were speaking to himself.

"You mean those young idiots who sit in Whites Club drinking too much claret and have nothing better to do than make stupid bets?" Malvina said scornfully. "I suppose you were an odds-on favourite."

"I was!" the Duke said bitterly. "When you refused Waddington they were quite certain you were waiting for a Duke."

"Well, I am not!" Malvina replied. "And you can tell your friends there are plenty of better uses for their money than wasting it on bets which concern me!"

She walked out of the Drawing-Room as she spoke, shutting the door sharply behind her.

As she went up a very impressive staircase towards her bed-room she told herself it was intolerable.

She was rich.

So it seemed that everybody in London apparently had nothing to do but speculate as to whom she would marry.

She went along the corridor and opened the door to the *Boudoir*.

She knew her grandmother would be resting after luncheon.

The Dowager Countess of Daresbury was sitting on a sofa in the window.

Her legs were covered by an exquisitely embroidered Chinese shawl.

She looked up when her granddaughter entered and smiled at her.

"Well," she asked, "do I congratulate you?"

"Certainly not!" Malvina replied. "I have told the Duke that I am not interested in his title, and I presume he will now take himself back to London!"

The Dowager Countess gave a little cry.

"You refused him? Oh, Malvina, how can you be so foolish?"

10

Malvina sat down beside the sofa.

The sunshine coming through the windows touched the gold in her hair, which seemed to spring into life.

Looking at her, the Dowager Countess thought it was quite unnecessary that she should be so beautiful, and, at the same time, so very rich!

It really seemed unfair.

Malvina did not speak, and after a moment the Dowager said:

"You know, dearest child, you are now twenty, and you missed the whole of last year because you were in mourning for your father. You cannot delay your decision for too long."

"Why not?" Malvina asked abruptly.

Her grandmother looked surprised.

"But surely you wish to be married?"

"Eventually," Malvina replied, "but not to one of those impoverished aristocrats whose only interest in me is that I have millions of Papa's money which he made by hard work."

Now the Dowager Countess's lips tightened for a moment.

She had always thought it unfortunate that while her son-in-law was undoubtedly a Gentleman, although not an aristocrat, he had made his money from trade.

His activities had taken place in the East.

So no one was quite certain how he had become the great Ship Owner, superlative trader, and undoubtedly a financial genius.

He was known jokingly as Mr. Ten Percent,

11

which was what he received from each new project.

However, it was not expected of a Gentleman.

The Countess and her husband had been deeply disappointed when their daughter had insisted on marrying Magnamus Maulton.

She had been wildly and overwhelmingly in love.

Once she got to know him, the Dowager had to admit that Magnamus was a very attractive man.

He had a masculinity, besides what the servants called "a honeyed tongue."

The two qualities combined inevitably fascinated a young girl.

He had swept Lady Elizabeth off her feet.

They were married in haste, which was regrettable.

Then Magnamus had taken her away to the East, where she was undoubtedly supremely happy.

They had returned to England only six years before, when Magnamus had bought a large, impressive house for his wife.

It was near enough to London for him to be able to keep in touch with all his business activities overseas.

The stories of how rich he was preceded him, and of course his wife was the daughter of the Earl of Daresbury!

Therefore it was not surprising that every door in Mayfair was open to him.

A year ago, tragedy changed Magnamus

Maulton's luck overnight.

His wife, whom he adored, died of a fever which no one could diagnose.

It seemed to the Doctors to be more fitted to the East than to England.

Then it was learnt that the same fever was raging in the Docks.

It had undoubtedly been carried in some of the ships which sailed from the Far East to bring spices, silks, and a dozen other commodities to the Port of London.

It must have been in the Docks that Magnamus Maulton, after so many years in the East, caught the same fever that had killed his wife.

Almost before Malvina realised what was happening, she found herself an orphan.

She wept bitterly in the large, empty house.

She wished she could have died with her father and mother.

It was her grandmother, the Dowager Countess, who had made her realise that life was very precious.

Also, as a great heiress, for her father had left her everything he possessed, she could find it very enjoyable.

The Dowager Countess left the Dower House where she was living since her son had inherited the title.

She came to Maulton Park to chaperon Malvina.

They spent the months of mourning in the country.

Malvina rode the superb horses her father had bought, and gradually got over the shock of his death.

Finally they opened the house in Berkeley Square which Magnamus Maulton had bought.

Malvina was a sensation overnight.

Everybody had talked of her father and the huge fortune he possessed!

They therefore expected his heir to be financially attractive, whatever her appearance.

What they did not expect was that Malvina should be undoubtedly the most beautiful girl that any critical Beau had ever seen.

Young aristocrats with empty pockets rushed to make her acquaintance.

She received five proposals the first fortnight she was in London.

After that they became monotonously frequent.

There were Baronets, Peers, and Earls.

For two weeks the betting was heaviest on a Marquess who was finding it hard to keep his race-horses, his fox-hounds, and a very expensive mistress at the same time.

Malvina refused them all, and it was the Marquess who said disagreeably when she turned him down:

"I suppose you are waiting for Wrexham! What woman could refuse to be a Duchess?"

He walked out of the room as he spoke and slammed the door behind him.

Malvina sighed.

Then she had gone riding and had not thought of him again.

She and her grandmother had come down to the country for Easter.

When the Duke of Wrexham was announced by the Butler, she knew exactly why he had followed her.

If the Marquess had just a slight chance of being accepted, the Duke had none.

She had sat next to him at various dinners in London, and danced with him at almost every Ball.

She found he was undoubtedly rather stupid.

He had little to talk about except himself.

She had not been surprised that her grandmother favoured his suit.

The Dowager had opposed her mother's wedding because her father had not been of any social consequence.

"Blue blood goes with blue blood!" was the rule for all aristocrats.

Magnamus Maulton, when he became so rich, was forgiven and more or less taken into the bosom of the family.

There were, however, still aunts and cousins and their friends who said in lowered voices:

"My dear, we must never talk about it, but he did make his money in trade!"

But Magnamus himself thought it an immense joke.

"They disapprove of me," he told his daughter laughingly. "However, they always have their hands out whenever I appear!"

"I have noticed that," Malvina said.

"I can understand it," her father had replied good-humouredly. "And as I have it, I give them what they want — why not?"

Malvina was determined to follow his example.

At the same time, she did not intend to give the Duke, or anyone else — herself.

Now she smiled a little mockingly as her grandmother said tentatively:

"You do not think, dearest child, that you might reconsider your decision where the Duke of Wrexham is concerned?"

Malvina got to her feet.

"No, Grandmama, and as I am very happy with you, why should there be any hurry for me to have a husband?"

She kissed her grandmother affectionately, and said:

"Now I am going riding, and I shall think of how beautiful the country is, and forget about men."

She went from the *Boudoir* as she spoke, and her grandmother sighed.

She loved Malvina.

She wished to see her happily settled with a husband to look after her vast fortune, and children to inherit it.

Malvina went to her own bed-room, where her maid was waiting to help her on with her riding-habit.

It was a pretty and very expensive one.

Made of a heavy blue silk which matched her eyes, it was trimmed with a white braid.

There was a lace-trimmed petticoat to wear beneath it, and her boots were soft and comfortable.

She did not wear a spur.

Her father had taught her years before how to control the most obstreperous horse without a whip and without the cruelty of a spur.

When she was dressed she ran downstairs.

She was not thinking of the Duke, but of her favourite horse, Dragonfly, who was waiting for her outside.

One groom was holding Dragonfly's bridle while another groom was riding on a horse that was almost equally as spectacular as hers.

Malvina was helped into the saddle, but, as the mounted groom was ready to follow her, she said:

"I do not require you this afternoon, Harris. I wish to ride alone."

Harris, who was a middle-aged man, looked at her in consternation.

He knew it would be hopeless to argue.

He therefore turned his horse to ride back to the stables while Malvina set off down the drive.

She rode across the Park to where there was some flat meadowland.

She took Dragonfly at the fastest pace of which he was capable.

Only when they had ridden a long way from

the house did she let him go more slowly.

Although she did not wish to admit it to herself, the interview with the Duke had upset her.

She did not like to think of the young men in Whites, Boodles, and the other Clubs in St. James's losing money because she had said "No."

Their behaviour made her feel degraded.

She knew it would have infuriated her father.

She found herself wondering if London was worth it.

Were the Balls that took place there every night really so amusing?

Was the approval or disapproval of the Dowagers who sat on a dais criticising everybody of real importance?

"What do I want? What do I desire of life?" she asked herself.

A bird rose ahead of her, frightened by her approach, and rose into the sky.

'That is what I want,' she thought, 'to be free, to be untrammelled.'

She knew that what marriage would bring her would be a prison.

However enjoyable, it would still be a prison from which she could not escape.

She rode on.

Now just ahead of her was the wood which bordered her estate.

It had been a bone of contention between her father and Lord Flore, who was their nearest neighbour.

Magnamus Maulton had bought the house

and the land surrounding it, both of which were in bad repair.

He understood that the wood had been included on the map with his Deeds.

Lord Flore, however, insisted that the wood was his.

He asserted over and over again that he had never sold an inch of his estate, and had no intention of doing so now.

The two men had argued with each other through their Solicitors until Magnamus Maulton had died.

Then Malvina had learned that three months later, Lord Flore had followed him.

She had not been particularly interested except that she was told that Flore Priory, which she had never visited, was empty.

There was no longer a claimant to what was now called "Wild Wood."

While the arguments over it were taking place, Magnamus Maulton had warned his game-keepers to keep out of the wood.

It was Malvina who found it entrancing.

This was one place on her father's perfectly kept three-thousand-acre estate that was left as Nature had intended it.

There were innumerable jays, magpies, stoats, weasels, and red squirrels, besides as many rabbits that made a continual rustle in the under-growth.

In the long months when she was in mourning and missed her father and mother unbearably,

Malvina would go into the wood every day.

There she felt that the birds and animals understood what she was feeling.

She knew that her grandmother loved her.

Her other relatives of the Daresbury family were always arriving, ostensibly to cheer her up.

But she was well aware that what they were really interested in was how she spent her money.

In Wild Wood she felt her father near her and laughing at the respectful way in which she was treated.

"I miss you, Papa . . . how I miss you!" Malvina thought now as she entered the wood.

She rode along the moss-covered twisting paths which led to the centre of it.

She knew only her father would understand why she had refused the Duke as well as all the other men who had proposed to her in the last three months.

She told herself that whatever her grandmother might say, she had no intention of marrying anyone.

"Why should I have a husband controlling my money, giving me orders, and trying to make me obey him?" she asked defiantly.

She rode on, hearing the rabbits scuttle away at her approach.

The squirrels were chattering in the trees in case she had come to steal their nuts.

In the centre of the wood there was a small pond that was fed in some mysterious way by a spring.

It was always full of clear sparkling water.

There were yellow kingcups already in bloom, and in the rough ground surrounding it there were primroses and white and purple violets.

Malvina dismounted and knotted Dragonfly's reins so that he could search for tufts of grass.

She knew he would come when she called him.

Pulling off her riding-hat, she sat down on a fallen tree which lay beside the pond.

Sitting there, the magic of the wood made her forget everything but the beauty of it.

In the distance she heard the cuckoo and overhead a small bird was singing.

Then suddenly there was a disturbance, and she realised that Dragonfly was rearing up between the fir trees.

She ran towards him, thinking as she did so that he must have been stung.

When she reached him he was rearing up and down.

She saw that what had upset him had caused him to move so violently that the knot she had tied on his reins had come undone.

Now he had them thrown over his head and had somehow got them under his front legs.

"It is all right . . . it is all right," she assured him soothingly, knowing he would listen to her voice. "Whatever hurt you will not do so again."

Dragonfly, however, was affronted.

He became even more entangled by the reins until Malvina wondered desperately what she should do.

Then, unexpectedly, a man's voice said:

"Let me help you."

"I think my horse has been stung," Malvina answered without turning round.

The man reached out and, taking Dragonfly by the bridle, pulled him clear of the brambles in which he was standing.

Then he said sharply:

"Hold your horse while I get the reins free. Surely, you silly girl, you know enough to knot them before you turn him loose?"

Malvina was so surprised at the way he spoke that she raised her eyes to look at her rescuer.

As she did so, she realised he was a Gentleman, if a somewhat unconventional one.

He was not wearing a hat, and his stock was tied loosely round his neck.

His clothes obviously came from a good tailor.

But when she could see his face she realised he was a Stranger.

In fact, he looked different from anyone she had ever seen before.

Dragonfly was now behaving more quietly, although his muscles were quivering as if with indignation at the way he had been treated.

The Stranger knotted his reins together firmly. Then he said severely:

"That is how you do it!"

"That was how I *did* do it!" Malvina answered coldly.

"But not very efficiently!"

"Thank you for your help!" Malvina said. "I was fortunate you were here, but may I point out

22

that you are in fact trespassing?"

"Trespassing?" the Stranger exclaimed, raising his eye-brows. "That is exactly what I was about to say to you!"

Malvina's eyes widened. Then she said:

"You . . . cannot mean . . . you are not . . . ?"

". . . the 'Black Sheep'?" the Stranger finished. "Or perhaps you would prefer 'The Prodigal Son' for whom, however, there is no 'fatted calf'!"

"You are . . . Lord Flore?"

"I am! And I imagine, as you are claiming the wood, that you are the 'Heartless Heiress!' "

Malvina stared at him, and he added:

"Forgive me if I sound rude, but ever since I returned to England two weeks ago, everybody I meet has nothing else to talk about but you."

Although she thought he was impertinent, Malvina laughed.

"I do not think that is a compliment!"

"Why not? All women want to be talked about."

"Then I must be the exception."

"I rather doubt it," Lord Flore replied, "and I find it hard to believe that you are here alone."

He looked around him.

"Where are your escorts, the *Aides-de-Camp*, the grooms, and, of course, the disconsolate suitors?"

Malvina's eyes flashed.

"Now you are being insulting!"

"If I am, then I apologise," he said disarmingly,

"but I expected you to be hung with diamonds, and at least riding on a saddle of pure gold!"

"You are ridiculous!" Malvina retorted. "And I should have thought you would have something more important to think about than me, considering the condition of your house and estate!"

Lord Flore's lips tightened, and in a very distant voice he said:

"That is true, but I am not certain what I can do about it."

"Perhaps you should sell the place," Malvina suggested. "I believe the Priory is very beautiful!"

"It is," he agreed. "At the same time, the last person I would sell it to is you!"

Again Malvina thought he was being rude, but because she was curious she could not help asking:

"Why not?"

"Because, Miss Maulton, you would undoubtedly change the mellow beauty of the ages into something unpleasantly modern and endeavour to imprint your personality on it, perhaps by signing every brick with your initials!"

Malvina stiffened.

"I think," she said slowly, "that you are the rudest man I have ever met!"

"I prefer the word 'frank.' "

"There is often very little difference between the two."

"Few women like the truth," Lord Flore remarked.

"That is untrue," Malvina argued, "but as you are obviously so prejudiced, there is no point in our discussing it any further!"

She thought as she spoke that she ought to ride away with dignity.

The difficulty was that they were both holding on to Dragonfly's bridle and talking across his back.

When she was alone, Malvina always mounted her horse by standing on a fallen tree.

Dragonfly knew what was expected of him and would stand still as she climbed into the saddle.

Now she felt this would be undignified with Lord Flore watching them.

But the last thing she wanted was for him to lift her into the saddle, which he would undoubtedly feel obliged to do.

For a moment there was silence.

Then Malvina said:

"I must thank Your Lordship for your help, and I am sure you wish to be on your way. I should not have taken up so much of your time."

Lord Flore laughed.

"Very nicely put! Do you, when you refuse your ardent suitors, speak to them in that decisive tone?"

Malvina pulled at Dragonfly's bridle, deciding that she would walk away, leading the horse.

Lord Flore, however, hung on to the bridle from the other side.

"Not so fast!" he said. "While you are here,

perhaps we could discuss once and for all the ownership of this much-contested wood?"

"How do you know about that?" Malvina asked. "I have always been told that you left home just before we came to live at the Park, and your father 'cut you off without a penny'!"

The story went that Shelton Flore, as he was then, had not left alone.

He had taken abroad with him the very attractive wife of one of their neighbours.

The scandalised County had learnt that when her husband died a year later, having refused to divorce her, she had married again, but not the man with whom she had run away.

The gossip about it and Shelton Flore's departure had been talked about incessantly.

When Magnamus Maulton and his wife moved into the house they re-christened "Maulton Park," everyone who called on them had something to add to the story.

In fact, Malvina could remember her father saying:

"I am tired of hearing about this obstreperous young man. One would think he was the only man in the world who had 'sown his wild oats.'"

"I rather agree with you," his wife had answered, "at the same time, Lord Flore does not make it easy for his son to return home. Yet I think, although he would not admit it, that he is rather a lonely man."

"Well, he certainly has no wish for our company, unless we concede him the right to the wood!" Magnamus Maulton replied. "And as a matter of principle, it is something I have no intention of doing."

Malvina's father and mother ceased to talk about Shelton Flore's outrageous behaviour.

But to the servants it was a wild, romantic tale which they repeated and repeated.

Because the two estates were side by side, it was impossible for the families who worked on them not to be closely related.

In the last three years Magnamus Maulton's estate was a perfect example of good farming and housing.

Flore Priory was exactly the opposite.

The labourers who were dismissed because there was no money to pay them came begging to Magnamus Maulton to employ them.

The Priory estate was left unfarmed.

There were rumours that the house itself was falling about its owner's ears.

"Master Shelton should come home and look after things!" the old people in the village said over and over again.

But there was no sign of "Master Shelton."

The Lord Lieutenant said to Magnamus Maulton:

"I think that young man is behaving disgracefully! I wrote and told him that his father was ill and that he should come home, but I have never received a reply."

Yet now, unexpectedly, the new Lord Flore was there!

But it was a year after his father had been buried and the Priory left deserted.

Because she wanted to know the answer, Malvina asked:

"Why did you not come back sooner?"

"I have already been asked that question a few hundred times," he replied, "and the answer is quite simple — I was in an inaccessible part of a country where letters could not reach me. It was not until two months ago that I came back to civilisation to learn that my father was dead."

"I do not think anybody thought that is what had happened," Malvina said. "They merely imagined you were not interested in knowing he was ill."

"I have never expected anyone to think anything but the worst of me!" Lord Flore replied. "I 'kicked over the traces' and make no apology for doing so."

"That sounds rather 'uppish,' " Malvina said.

Lord Flore laughed.

"That is exactly what I am, and thank you for giving me the right description of it."

"Does that mean that you have come home with a fortune?" Malvina asked. "It is what I am told the Priory and your estate needs."

"Oh, God, no!" Lord Flore exclaimed. "As I have already told you, I am the 'Prodigal Son,' and I have enjoyed eating the husks but have nothing to show for it."

"Then what are you going to do?" Malvina enquired.

Lord Flore shrugged his shoulders.

Then he said:

"The only suggestion I have been offered so far is that I should marry you!"

Malvina was about to give a cry of protest, but he went on:

"Do not worry! You are quite safe! I would rather marry Medusa — snakes and all!"

Malvina was so surprised that she asked:

"Why should you say that?"

"Because, my dear Miss Maulton, I would have to pay too heavily for your money-bags. And if you will forgive me saying so, you are the type of woman I most abominate!"

"I do not have to stay here listening to you talking to me like that!" Malvina exclaimed angrily.

"You asked me a question, and I told you the truth!" Lord Flore said. "And for Heaven's sake, be sensible enough to talk intelligently about yourself without expecting to be effusively flattered!"

"I do not expect *that!*" Malvina objected.

"Then stop bucking and rearing like your horse at everything I say!" Lord Flore retorted.

Malvina gave a little gasp as he went on:

"It would make things much easier between us if we were truthful with each other. I promise you I am telling you the truth when I say I do not wish to marry you, and have no intention of giving you the satisfaction of turning me down like that wretched Duke, whom you have just dismissed."

Malvina looked surprised and exclaimed:

"You know about that?"

"I was in Whites Club yesterday and saw Wrexham look at the Betting-Book with satisfaction, and heard his friends wishing him luck. It was quite obvious he thought he had already passed the winning-post, and had the Gold Cup in his hand."

Malvina could not help laughing.

She thought Lord Flore was the rudest man she had ever met in her whole life.

At the same time, she had to admit that he was amusing.

"Now that we have established," she said, "that you do not wish to marry me, which I have to admit is a great relief, what are you going to do?"

"I thought, as a neighbour, if we are prepared to ignore the way our fathers sharpened their teeth on each other, you might help me."

"In what way?" Malvina asked.

"Well, as it is quite obvious, in the time-honoured manner of such situations, what I have come home to," Lord Flore replied, "I will either have to sell everything I possess, which will fetch very little, or marry an heiress."

Malvina stared at him.

"I thought that was the one thing you had decided not to do!"

"I do not wish to marry *you!*" Lord Flore answered. "You are far too aggressive. And, quite frankly, I do not want the type of wife who figures in the Betting-Book at Whites, and whose name is bandied about by every young waster who has nothing better to do."

Malvina's eyes flashed, and he said:

"Now, now, do not take it the wrong way. Again, I am only telling you the truth."

"Then what *do* you want?" she asked with an edge on her voice.

"I want someone soft, sweet, and feminine," he replied, "who will think I am wonderful, and understand that I want to spend her money in restoring the Priory, and not on riotous parties or currying favour with a lot of idiotic aristocrats because they have titles."

There was silence. Then he said:

"I have been told of all the innovations your father introduced to improve the smooth running of the farms, but, of course, he could afford it! As I want to afford it too, I must have money."

"And you want me to find you an heiress?" Malvina asked incredulously.

"Money goes to money," Lord Flore said, "and I cannot imagine anyone in a better position to find me the type of woman who would enjoy the country and keep me from yearning for the high mountains, the deep oceans, besides the thrill of finding lost Temples and ruined Palaces in strange, outlandish places."

"Is that what you have been doing?" Malvina asked.

"Amongst other things," he said, "and if my elders and betters consider it a mis-spent youth,

31

all I can say is that I do not regret a minute of it!"

"I suppose I can understand that," Malvina said.

"I must admit," Lord Flore went on, "when I have been riding on an obstreperous mule, or a yak that will not go above a snail's pace up a perilous mountain with a sharp wind in my face, I have sometimes yearned for a horse like yours!"

He indicated Dragonfly as he went on:

"But I suppose it is something I shall never be able to afford."

For the first time, Malvina glanced at his horse that was cropping the grass in a clearing.

It was certainly an inferior animal, and she guessed it was the only one left in the Priory stable.

On an impulse she said:

"Because I have been in London and there has been no one at home, my horses are under-exercised. If you would like to borrow one whenever you need one, you would actually be doing me a favour."

Lord Flore laughed.

"That is certainly being magnanimous, Miss Maulton, and let me respond by saying that I accept your offer with pleasure. At the same time, I offer you the freedom of my wood!"

"It is not *your* wood . . . !" Malvina began.

Then she laughed.

"We cannot go through all that again! Let us leave it as a 'No-man's-land' which is available to both of us, but please do not kill what my keepers think of as vermin, or the birds."

Lord Flore spread out his hands.

"Let me make you a present of all of it!" he said. "And also the wasp, or whatever insect it was that stung your horse."

Malvina laughed again, then she let go of Dragonfly's bridle and said:

"If you will help me into the saddle, I must go home. I hope you will call on my grandmother, who is living with me, both here and in London."

"I shall be delighted to do so," Lord Flore replied, "but as the Flores have lived in this part of the world for three-hundred years, I think it is my prerogative to invite you first to the Priory."

He walked round Dragonfly as he spoke to stand near to Malvina as he said:

"Will you give me the pleasure of taking tea with me to-morrow? I doubt if you will get anything palatable to eat, but I would like to show you my home."

"I should love that," Malvina said. "To be honest, I have always been curious about the Priory, and annoyed that your father and mine were not on speaking terms."

Then she gave a little cry.

"I have just remembered," she said, "that my grandmother and I had planned that we would go back to London to-morrow and have accepted engagements both for a luncheon and a dinner-party on Wednesday."

"In which case," Lord Flore said, "you had better come and see the Priory now, otherwise it could be weeks, if not months, before I have the honour of your presence again!"

There was a mocking note in his voice which she did not miss.

She thought if she was not so curious about his house she would ride away now.

She could wait for perhaps a month or more before she accepted his invitation.

Then she decided that however tiresome he might be and, she thought, rude, she wanted to see the Priory.

"I will come now," she said, "but you do realise I cannot stay long."

"Of course," he agreed, "you may find that just a quick glance is quite enough!"

It was not what she expected him to say.

Then he picked her up in his arms and deposited her on Dragonfly's back.

He unknotted the reins, then walked away to his own horse.

As he did so, she realised that he was very athletic.

His broad shoulders and narrow hips gave him a very distinctive physique.

She thought as she had before that he certainly looked very different from any other man she had seen.

He was not exactly handsome, but he had what she thought of as a raffish face, rather as she expected a pirate to look.

She was, however, sure that in real life he would be different.

Lord Flore had dark hair and rather pronounced eye-brows.

She already knew there was a twinkle in his eye when he was being rude.

Or was he deliberately provocative?

She did not understand him, and she thought a great many other people would feel the same.

'I expect,' she thought as they emerged from the wood, 'he is just as bad and irresponsible as he was when he ran away with somebody else's wife!'

chapter two

They rode out of the wood and across a field.

A few minutes later Malvina had her first sight of the Priory.

It was so lovely that she gave a gasp.

It was far bigger than she had expected, even though she had learnt that it had been added to considerably over the generations.

Because he had been interested in his neighbours, her father had told her about the Priory.

After the Dissolution of the Monasteries in the reign of Henry VIII, it had become a private house.

When Queen Mary came to the throne, however, it was returned to the Benedictine monks.

Then her sister Elizabeth changed everything again.

The monks were persecuted, and the first Lord Flore, who was a Statesman at Court, became the owner of the Priory.

He had its name changed to his own, and the Flores had lived there ever since.

It was a great stone building and looked very beautiful in the sunshine.

Only when she drew nearer could Malvina see that many of the windows in the upstairs rooms were cracked and the bricks needed pointing.

There was moss and weeds growing on the long flight of steps which led up to the front-door.

Lord Flore did not say anything.

He merely dismounted and lifted Malvina from Dragonfly's back.

He knotted the reins as he had before and left the two horses to graze on the unkept lawn, where the grass had grown high.

Then, as they walked up the steps to the front-door, he said:

"The only consolation is that my father never sold anything in the house, and I think if I did so now, he would haunt me!"

"I am sure he would!" Malvina replied.

They had walked straight into the huge Hall.

She knew it was where the monks had dined and where they had extended their hospitality to anyone who was in need.

The long refectory table was exquisitely carved, and would have easily seated thirty or more people.

There were oak chairs to match it, and a medieval fireplace which would burn the whole trunk of a tree.

The diamond-paned windows were intact, but badly in need of cleaning.

The same could be said of the pictures which covered most of the walls.

"This is the Great Hall," Lord Flore said unnecessarily.

They walked through it, and he showed Malvina a number of smaller rooms.

They were all decorated with what she realised were portraits of his ancestors down the ages.

It also contained what she was sure was a number of antique and very valuable pieces of furniture.

She glanced at one cabinet made of different woods, with gilt feet and handles.

She knew it would fetch a large sum in a Sale room.

Lord Flore must have read her thoughts, because he said firmly:

"The answer is 'No'!"

"In which case," Malvina said, "I shall have to find you an heiress!"

"That is what I have told you to do."

"It should not be difficult," she murmured. "Any woman would find it fascinating to bring this lovely house back to the perfection it once had."

"I remember that is how it looked in my grandfather's time," Lord Flore said.

Malvina raised her eye-brows.

"Then what happened to all your money?"

"I suppose a truthful reply would be to say that I spent quite a lot of it. But actually it was the war. It crippled my father as it crippled so many ancestral estates all over England."

"The farmers did well," Malvina said, thinking he was showing his ignorance.

"I agree," Lord Flore replied, "but a large number went into bankruptcy when hostilities were over, and any money that was invested abroad was irretrievably lost."

Malvina thought of her father and said:

"That is not true of everybody."

"Your father was an exception, and in the East, where he made his money, he was almost worshipped for his brilliance."

"Did you know my father?" Malvina asked.

"I met him several times," Lord Flore replied, "and he was very kind and helpful to me."

Malvina smiled.

"My father was helpful to everybody; and now that you tell me that, I am sure he would have liked you to ride his horses."

"You could not say anything that would give me greater pleasure," Lord Flore replied, "and now I will show you two more rooms before I take you home."

"I am quite safe riding alone," Malvina replied.

"At the same time, it is something you should not do."

She put up her hands.

"Now, do not start, because I said we were friends, ordering me about! I am sick of being told what I can or cannot do, and I intend to have my own way."

Lord Flore smiled. Then he said:

"Now you understand why I do not wish to

marry you. You had much better accept the Duke. He would be stupid enough to let you behave abominably and say nothing about it."

"While you, no doubt, would have a great deal to say!" Malvina retorted.

"Naturally!" Lord Flore replied. "And after a week or two I expect I should find I would have to beat you into submission!"

His eyes were twinkling, but she had the feeling that "there was many a true word spoken in jest."

"I will find you," she replied quickly, "that quiet, complacent, half-witted little mouse you want as a wife! I am sure there are plenty of them about!"

"One will be quite enough," Lord Flore replied.

Because Malvina was determined to have the last word, she said:

"Do not be too sure of that! If you run through her money at the same rate as you ran through your own, you may need a continuous stream of them!"

He laughed.

Then, as if he thought they had said enough, he led the way back to the front-door.

Malvina called Dragonfly.

He raised his head and came trotting back to her obediently.

Lord Flore helped her into the saddle.

Then he collected his own horse and they rode back the way they had come.

There was no sign of anyone working in the fields through which they passed which were unploughed and un-sown.

The contrast when they came through the wood into the Maulton estate was very obvious.

Lord Flore would have been blind if he had not seen the young wheat sprouting in one field, while another was sown with barley.

Even the trees in the orchard, having been well pruned, were showing the promise of being fruitful.

There were no broken boughs left under the oak trees in the Park, and the lawns near the house were smooth and green.

The Spring flowers were in bloom, the shrubs showing the colour of their buds.

Every window in the great house was polished until it shone like a diamond.

The front steps had been scrubbed until they were spotless.

Only as they approached a little nearer did Malvina see a smart Phaeton.

Drawn by four horses, it was just moving from the front of the house in the direction of the stables.

As she looked at it questioningly, Lord Flore said:

"I think another optimistic admirer has arrived, and it is a good thing I did not keep you any longer!"

"I am not expecting anyone!" Malvina replied almost angrily.

It annoyed her that he should think she had an assignation which she had not admitted.

Then, as she took another look at the Phaeton before it disappeared, she guessed who was her caller.

She had no wish to see him.

Sir Mortimer Smythe was the first baronet who had proposed to her when she had arrived in London.

He was a thick-set, rather unattractive man.

He paid her compliments which she knew were exaggerated.

She had the feeling there was something unpleasant about him.

He had proposed to her very ardently.

When she had refused his offer of marriage he said:

"I am well aware that I am the first of many, but I assure you, Miss Maulton, I am not easily disposed of and I shall continue to press my suit."

"It will be useless, Sir Mortimer," Malvina replied.

"That remains to be seen," he answered. "In the meantime, may I tell you how beautiful you are, and how passionately I want you to be my wife!"

He kissed her hand.

When his lips actually touched her skin she felt herself shudder.

"I do not like Sir Mortimer Smythe," she had told her grandmother.

"He comes from a respected family," the Dowager replied. "At the same time, he is too old for you, being at least thirty-six, and there are some strange stories about him."

"What are they?" Malvina enquired.

But her grandmother would not say any more.

Now she hoped that the Dowager Countess would have come downstairs for tea.

Sometimes when she rested after luncheon they had tea together in her *Boudoir*.

Then she would only come down for dinner.

In which case, Malvina thought, she would have to see Sir Mortimer alone.

On an impulse she said to Lord Flore, who had not dismounted and was just about to ride away:

"Will you come in? I want you to meet my grandmother."

"As you already have a visitor," he replied, "I do not think I would be very welcome."

"I am asking you as . . . a favour."

He raised his eye-brows, and his eyes were twinkling.

"That is different!" he said. "I had the idea you were giving me an order!"

"You are being ridiculous!" Malvina snapped.

He dismounted and handed his reins to the groom, who was already holding Dragonfly.

Then they walked up the steps together to where the Butler and two footmen wearing her father's livery were waiting.

"Sir Mortimer Smythe's in the Drawing-

43

Room, Miss Malvina," the Butler said. "Her Ladyship has not yet come downstairs."

"Then we will have tea immediately, Newman," Malvina replied, "unless the Gentlemen would prefer champagne."

"Very good, Miss."

He walked across the room and into the hall to open the door into the Drawing-Room.

It was a large and very impressive room and overlooked the rose-garden at the back of the house.

Lord Flore followed her.

Malvina found Sir Mortimer Smythe standing with his back to the fire.

This was lit late in the afternoon because the evenings could be chilly.

He smiled as he saw Malvina and hurried across the room towards her, saying:

"Most beautiful Lady, I could stay away no longer! When I heard you had left London, the whole place was desolate without you!"

"My grandmother and I are returning to-morrow," Malvina said in a cold voice. "I do not know whether you know my neighbour, Lord Flore?"

"I heard you were back, Flore!" Sir Mortimer said in an uncompromising tone. "Are things as bad as you expected?"

Malvina realised he was being unpleasant, but then Lord Flore replied:

"Worse, but let me point out, it is entirely my business!"

"But of course!" Sir Mortimer replied. "And how wise of you to make our charming and beautiful hostess sorry for you."

Lord Flore walked towards the fireplace.

"You seem to be very interested in my affairs," he said. "But I am wondering what has brought you here. It is quite a distance from London, unless you are staying in the neighbourhood?"

"As I have just told the lovely Miss Malvina, had you been listening," Sir Mortimer replied, "London is a barren desert without her, and I sought her as Jason sought the Golden Fleece."

"The covering of a sheep," Lord Flore said scathingly. "Hardly a very apt description of Miss Maulton!"

Sir Mortimer gave him a withering glance.

"If you are going to be as tiresome as you were before you went abroad," he said nastily, "it is a pity you ever came back!"

"I dare say quite a number of people will think that," Lord Flore replied blandly, "but how can I resist making the acquaintance of such an attractive neighbour as Miss Maulton?"

He looked at Malvina as he spoke.

She knew that he was deliberately provoking Sir Mortimer by insinuating that he was courting her.

She knew the supposition was correct when she saw the flash of anger in Sir Mortimer's dark eyes.

She felt she could read his thoughts.

He was thinking that if Lord Flore was in the

45

running and lived next door, he would have an unfair advantage over her other suitors.

Because she did not like Sir Mortimer and thought it was tiresome of him to have pursued her from London, she said:

"Of course, I am delighted, now that I have met Lord Flore, that we have managed to eliminate the disagreement which has unfortunately existed for years between his family and mine."

Sir Mortimer gave Lord Flore an angry glance before he replied:

"I hope your grandmother is aware of what you are doing."

Malvina did not have to answer.

At that moment Newman and two footmen came into the room with the tea.

There was the usual paraphernalia of a fine early Georgian silver tray on which was a kettle, a tea-pot, milk and cream jugs, and a sugar bowl.

There was also, as had been introduced in the reign of Queen Anne, a silver tea-caddy.

From it Malvina could spoon the tea into the pot once she had warmed it.

When this was set on the table, there were also hot scones, sandwiches, and a small and a large cake.

There was another which was covered with pink and white icing.

As Malvina busied herself with brewing the tea, Lord Flore took upon himself the duties of host.

He offered Sir Mortimer a hot scone.

46

He said abruptly:

"I will help myself!"

Malvina could feel the animosity vibrating from him.

She thought he was being needlessly aggressive.

She deliberately handed the cup of tea she had poured out for him to Lord Flore, saying:

"Will you please give this to Sir Mortimer? He may need a little more milk than I have already added to it."

Lord Flore carried the cup and saucer to Sir Mortimer's side.

He set it down on a small table.

As he did so, Malvina gave an exclamation and said:

"Oh, I forgot! Perhaps you would rather have a glass of wine after your long journey. You will certainly need one before you return."

"I thought, as I had come so far," Sir Mortimer replied, "I might ask you to be generous enough to give me dinner, and, if your grandmother is resting, we could be alone."

He gave Lord Flore a sharp glance as he spoke, but before Malvina could reply, Lord Flore said:

"That is a most improper suggestion, Smythe, as you well know! It would be quite impossible for Miss Maulton to dine with a man without a chaperone!"

"My dear Flore, you are sadly out of date," Sir Mortimer replied. "In London, I quite agree it might cause a certain amount of gossip. But here

47

in the country things are different, and, after all, I have come a long way."

"Without an invitation!" Lord Flore remarked.

"What has that to do with you?" Sir Mortimer snarled.

Malvina thought things had gone far enough.

"I am quite capable," she said in a crushing tone, "of answering Sir Mortimer's request myself, and it is quite simply — 'No'!"

She paused before she went on:

"It is not that I am worried about the conventions, but quite frankly I came to the country to rest, and as we are returning to London tomorrow, I intend to go to bed early."

She spoke decisively, as if there could be no possible argument about her decision.

As she finished speaking she realised that Lord Flore's eyes were twinkling.

There was a mocking twist to his lips.

It told her he was thinking that she was certainly not a soft, gentle little woman who needed to be looked after and protected.

Because it annoyed her, she said to Sir Mortimer in a more pleasant voice than she had used before:

"I expect, Sir Mortimer, we shall meet tomorrow night at the Ball which is being given at Devonshire House."

"You will give me the first dance?" Sir Mortimer asked.

"That I cannot promise," Malvina answered

quickly. "But I am sure you may have a dance sometime during the evening."

"You know it is something I shall be thinking about and looking forward to," Sir Mortimer said, "and if you break your promise, I shall feel like shooting myself!"

"Mind you do not miss!" Lord Flore remarked. "I remember in the past you were not exactly a 'crack shot' with a pistol!"

Sir Mortimer knew he was referring to a duel in which he had been defeated.

He flushed with anger.

Lord Flore, however, had risen to his feet.

Malvina knew he was about to go and leave her alone with Sir Mortimer.

Quickly she rose too.

"I think you must both excuse me now," she said. "I wish to run upstairs and see how my grandmother is. She has been asleep while I have been out riding and she likes to know when I am back."

She held out her hand to Lord Flore and added:

"Good-bye, Lord Flore, I shall not forget what I have promised to do for you."

"That is very kind, and of course I am extremely grateful," he replied.

She was well aware of what she was doing as she held out her hand to Sir Mortimer.

"Thank you for coming to see me," she said. "I hope you will not have too arduous a drive back to London."

"I would," he replied, "drive from John

o'Groats to Land's End to see you!"

His fingers tightened on hers.

Then, as she thought he would kiss it, she pulled her hand sharply away from him.

She hurried towards the door before either man could open it for her.

As she did so herself she turned back to say:

"Good-bye, and of course it has been delightful to see you both!"

She shut the Drawing-Room door and ran up the stairs.

At the same time, she wished she could be a fly on the wall to hear what the men she had left behind her were saying.

They were extremely acrimonious, as she might have expected.

Sir Mortimer glared at Lord Flore.

"I need not ask what you are doing here," he said angrily, "but I can tell you that better men than you have failed where the 'Heartless Heiress' is concerned."

"Is that who you are talking about?" Lord Flore asked. "My dear chap, I am so sorry for you!"

"I do not want your sympathy!" Sir Mortimer snapped. "I just want you to get out and stay out! We all know your reputation, and I cannot believe the Dowager Countess would allow her granddaughter to marry a Rake like you!"

Lord Flore deliberately sat down in a chair as if he had a right to do so, and crossed his legs.

He seemed very much at home, and he was

aware that it infuriated Sir Mortimer.

"I do not think," he said slowly, "that the Dowager or anyone else will have much say about who Malvina marries. She has her father's brain as well as some of his genius in getting what she wants out of life without anybody being able to prevent it."

Sir Mortimer was still for a moment.

Then he said:

"She has refused Wrexham, but if she is not after a Duke, what does she want?"

"You must ask her," Lord Flore answered, "but for the moment, I doubt if she knows herself!"

He saw Sir Mortimer's thin and rather unpleasant lips tighten, and he told himself he had said enough.

He rose from the chair, saying:

"Well, I must be on my way home. Good luck, Smythe! And of course, good hunting!"

He went from the room without looking back, but leaving the door open.

It told Sir Mortimer without words that he was expected to follow.

Lord Flore's horse had been taken to the stables, and although a footman offered to fetch it, he said he would go there himself.

He found it had been put in a stall and the Head Groom came hurrying towards him.

"Your horses are magnificent!" Lord Flore exclaimed, looking around him. "And Miss Maulton has given me permission to help you exercise them when I have the time."

The Head Groom touched his forelock.

"Noice t'see ye 'ome, Master Shelton! It's a sad state the Priory be in."

"It is indeed!" Lord Flore replied. "I believe I remember you!"

The groom grinned.

"Oi was a-workin' in yer stables, M'Lord, afore ye went off t' foreign parts."

"I thought I was not mistaken," Lord Flore said, "and your name is Hodgson."

The Head Groom beamed.

"Tha's roight, M'Lord! There wasn't enough 'orses after Y'Lordship 'ad left, so Oi comes 'ere to Mr. Maulton as third groom, but now Oi be the 'Ead."

"You have a fine lot of animals to look after."

Lord Flore paused. Then he asked:

"Is Miss Maulton riding to-morrow morning?"

"Seven o'clock, M'Lord, afore 'er leaves for Lonnon."

"Then I will be here at seven o'clock, Hodgson," Lord Flore said, "and give me the most spirited animal you have."

"Oi'll mak sure o' that, M'Lord."

Lord Flore held out his hand.

"Thank you, Hodgson, it is good to see you again."

"It's a soight fer sore eyes to see Yer Lordship, an' that's a fact!"

Having no idea what had been planned,

52

Malvina came down the stairs as the grandfather clock struck the hour.

She found not only Dragonfly waiting for her outside the door, but also Lord Flore on Thunderer, a black stallion.

He was rearing and bucking to show his independence.

For a moment Malvina stood at the top of the steps, watching.

She knew as she did so that she had never seen a man look better on a horse.

To-day Lord Flore was wearing a top-hat on the side of his dark hair and his stock was neatly tied.

His whip-cord riding-coat, which had obviously been worn for some time, fitted without a wrinkle.

His riding-boots shone like a mirror.

She wondered if he had polished them himself or had a valet to do it for him.

Then she remembered there had been no servants in evidence when she had visited the Priory yesterday.

She came down the steps.

Despite the difficulty he was having controlling Thunderer, Lord Flore raised his hat.

"Good-morning!" he said. "I hope you will permit me to accompany you."

"It appears I have little choice," Malvina replied.

But she was smiling as the groom helped her into the saddle.

They rode down the drive and turned towards the open land which led eventually to Wild Wood.

It was the best place for galloping.

By the time they had reached the wood, Malvina's cheeks were flushed and she was a little breathless.

She looked towards Lord Flore, who said:

"I cannot tell you how much I am enjoying riding one of the most magnificent horses I have ever mounted."

"Thunderer was Papa's favourite," Malvina said, "and I expect, as you are such a good rider, that is why Hodgson gave him to you."

"Now you are paying me compliments I really appreciate!" Lord Flore smiled.

They did not, however, waste time in talking but set off again.

They galloped alongside the wood on land that had been left fallow and was as good, Lord Flore thought, as any race-course.

He was just about to say this to Malvina as their horses settled down to a trot, when he exclaimed:

"I have an idea! But you will have to help me with it, for I could not do it without you."

"What is it?" she asked.

"I have often thought in the past that what this County lacked was a race-course. Suppose, between us, we constructed one? And if it was good enough, it would not only attract people who would spend a great deal of money here, but also provide employment for those on my estate I cannot afford to pay."

Malvina stared at him for a moment.

Then she said:

"Are you asking me to help you?"

"I have already said I could not do it without you," Lord Flore replied, "but make no mistake, every penny you expend will be repaid, even though I may at first have to borrow either from you, or from the Bank."

There was a bitter note in his voice and a hard look in his eyes as he added:

"I imagine the Bank would accept you as security, if they will not accept me."

"A race-course!" Malvina cried. "I think it is a wonderful idea! And you are quite right, the nearest course is miles away, and Papa used to complain that when he wanted to go racing he had to take almost a day to get there."

"We are near to London," Lord Flore said reflectively. "You could bring some of your father's horses from Newmarket, and there used to be several other race-horse owners in the County."

"There are at least three," Malvina said.

Then she gave a cry of joy.

"Oh, do start at once! It will be so exciting, and I only wish Papa had thought of it!"

"As you know it will please him, then you will know that you are not spending his money unnecessarily," Lord Flore said.

They talked it over for the rest of their ride,

then as they rode back to the house Malvina said:

"Put everything in hand immediately! I will tell Papa's Solicitor in London who has charge of my affairs what we are going to do, and to see that any money you require is made available to you straight away."

Lord Flore was silent for a moment.

Then he said:

"I have just thought, Malvina, and I cannot go on calling you Miss Maulton, that it would be a mistake for anyone to know at the moment that you are involved in this."

"Oh, but why?" Malvina asked.

"It would mean the gossips would talk about you and me, and as they know nothing to my advantage, it would be a mistake."

Malvina put her chin up in the air.

"I have never heard such nonsense! They will talk whatever I do or whatever I do not do, and if I want to help you build a race-course, then there is nothing they can do about it."

"Nothing!" Lord Flore agreed. "But I will not be instrumental in having you talked about in an even more vulgar manner than you are at the moment."

Malvina sighed.

"If you think you are going to make me become the quiet, gentle, crushed little heiress you wish to marry, you will be disappointed!"

She saw him scowl as she went on:

"I am your business partner, and the world

can say what it likes."

"You will do as I tell you," Lord Flore said sharply, "and that means you must speak about this to nobody until I allow you to do so."

"Are you really giving me orders?" Malvina questioned. "I have never heard such impertinence!"

"Stop being a spoilt little brat!" he said. "Try to understand that I am doing what your father would agree was best for you."

There was nothing Malvina could reply to this.

She knew in her heart he was right.

To talk about the race-course until it was a *fait accompli* would be to have the whole of the Social World chattering their heads off.

"Very well," she said grudgingly, "you win! But do not make a habit of ordering me about, or I will marry the Duke!"

"Do anything you like with him," Lord Flore retorted, "as long as you do not lend him your horses. He is heavy in the saddle, and cow-fisted with the reins!"

The way he spoke made Malvina laugh.

When finally Lord Flore left her and rode away to the stables to collect his own horse, Malvina wished she were not going to London.

She had a feeling that the parties, receptions, and Balls would seem "tame" after what was taking place in the country.

chapter three

Malvina was sitting at a desk writing a letter to Lord Flore.

She was writing to tell him what she had arranged with her Solicitor.

Any money he required should be lent to him.

She added that a representative of the firm would call on him within the next two days.

She had written the date and started: "Dear . . ." then she paused.

She was wondering, as he had called her "Malvina," whether she should call him by his Christian name, or continue to be formal.

She had the feeling he would laugh at her.

She therefore considered for a moment, then wrote: "Dear Neighbour and Partner . . ."

She was wondering what he would make of that, when the door opened and the Butler announced:

"The Earl of Andover, Miss!"

Malvina looked up quickly intending to say she was "not at home."

It was too late, for the Earl came into the room.

He was very smartly dressed, in fact, she thought he must be a Dandy because his cravat was so high it seemed impossible for him to move his neck.

His champagne-coloured pantaloons fitted tightly under a coat that had obviously been cut by Weston — the King's tailor.

His Hessian boots must, she thought, have been polished with champagne.

As he advanced towards her she felt he actually looked too elegant and over-dressed for a man.

She remembered when she had danced with him the night before that he had been very effusive with his compliments.

Now she had the uneasy feeling that he had called in order to propose to her.

She had only just returned from a large and rather stiff luncheon.

The hostess was so over-effusive that she was not surprised to find that the eldest son was seated on her right.

The youngest was on her left.

Both of them were somewhat unattractive.

She had been glad when her grandmother had said it was time to return home.

The Dowager had then gone upstairs to rest.

Malvina wondered how she could get rid of the Earl without once again having to refuse a proposal of marriage.

"I am so delighted to find you alone," he said as he bowed over her hand.

"I am afraid, My Lord, I am very busy," Malvina replied, "and therefore cannot spare any time from my duties."

"Please, do not turn me away," he begged.

He spoke in a surprisingly pleading tone, and as she looked at him she realised he was very young.

In fact, she guessed he was not much more than twenty-one.

She had the feeling that he was desperate.

"I can give you only a few minutes," she said in reply to his plea.

She would have moved towards the sofa by the mantelpiece if he had not held on to her hand.

"I have come to ask you," he said, "if you will do me the very great honour of becoming my wife."

Malvina tried to take her hand from his as she said:

"I think you already know the answer to that question."

"But — you must marry me — you must!" the Earl insisted. "Otherwise I will have to — kill myself!"

Malvina stared at him, thinking that he must be joking.

Then, seeing the anguished look in his eyes, she realised he was serious.

"You should not be thinking of doing anything so foolish," she remarked.

"It is not — foolish to me!" the Earl replied. "Please, Miss Maulton — marry me — I swear I will be the best — husband any woman ever — had!"

With some difficulty Malvina freed her hand.

She walked to the sofa and sat down.

Then, as the Earl followed her and sat beside her, she asked:

"Now, what is all this about? I do not believe anyone should propose marriage after such a short acquaintance."

"I know that," the Earl replied, "and you have every man in London at your feet — but I am an Earl and my family is an old one."

"When I do marry," Malvina said, "it will not be because my husband has a title."

"I heard you had refused Wrexham," the Earl said. "But — I just thought — because I am younger and would — do everything you wanted me to do — you might — accept me!"

"I think, actually," Malvina said, "you are too young to be married."

"I suppose I am," the Earl said unhappily, "but it is either a case of my — marrying or shooting myself!"

There was silence for a moment.

Then Malvina said in a kinder voice than she had used to most of her suitors:

"I suppose you are deeply in debt."

"I have — gambled away my last — penny!" the Earl said.

"How could you be so foolish?" Malvina enquired.

The Earl gave a deep sigh.

"When — my father died a year ago," he said, "I — came into the title — I had an offer for the — family house."

He paused.

Then, as if the words seemed to be jerked from him, he said:

"It was wrong — I knew it was wrong — but there was no money to keep it up — and I thought I would make my fortune in London and — buy another house to live in."

"And what happened?" Malvina asked.

"I — I thought the money would — last for ever!" the Earl said. "But now — I have — lost it all!"

Malvina knew without being told that he had been fascinated by the Beaux and Bucks.

When they were not racing they sat in their Clubs in St. James's Street, drinking and gambling.

Quite a number of them were very well off, and she could understand this stupid boy who wanted to shine amongst them.

Doubtless he would have been too shy to hold back when he realised he was losing at cards.

Her father had explained to her how the games of chance could have a magnetic attraction for men who had little to do.

When they had placed a lot of money on the turn of a card it was very difficult not to accept a challenge.

This meant doubling or trebling their stakes.

"I have been an — absolute fool — I know

that," the Earl went on, "and now I owe not only a dozen shop-keepers, who are — pressing me and will undoubtedly send me — to prison if I cannot pay — but I also owe a fortune in gaming debts!"

Malvina knew these were debts of honour.

If he was unable to pay them, he could be thrown out of his Club and be ostracised by his friends.

They would consider him a cad and no longer a Gentleman.

"What can you do?" she asked.

"If you will not — marry me," the Earl replied, "and I never expected you would, then I have a choice of putting a bullet in my head — or it will be — the river!"

He got up from the sofa as he spoke and moved to the window.

He stared out into the garden which was bright with tulips and daffodils, primroses and narcissi.

"Why did I ever leave the country?" he asked.

He was speaking more to himself than to Malvina, but she had a sudden idea.

She could hear Lord Flore saying:

" 'Your father was kind and very helpful to me.' "

Then there was her own voice replying:

" 'Papa always helped everyone.' "

"Come back, My Lord," she said aloud.

He turned from the window and walked back to the sofa.

She could see the tragic expression in his eyes, and she had the feeling he was not far from tears.

"Sit down," she said, "I have something to say to you."

He obeyed her rather carefully because his pantaloons were so tight.

"Tell me, My Lord," she began, "what else can you do besides gamble?"

The Earl thought for a moment.

Then he said:

"I can ride, but I cannot see myself making any money by doing that."

"You have no talents?"

"I tried to paint pictures when I was a boy," he said, "but I was not very good and I doubt if any-one would buy them."

There was a note of despair in his voice.

Malvina knew he was thinking of the very few shillings he might make out of anything he could do.

It would be a drop in the ocean in relation to his debts.

Then, as if he realised she was trying to help him, he said:

"I did two murals on the walls at home which my mother thought were — good, but I doubt if — anyone would — employ me."

"Murals?" Malvina exclaimed.

As she spoke she had a vision of the rooms in the Priory, of the paper peeling from the walls, the woodwork rotting for lack of paint, and the doors in the same condition.

"Are you prepared to work, and work hard?"

"I will do anything," the Earl said, "but what

is there for me to do?"

Malvina hesitated. Then she said:

"I will pay your debts if you will swear to me on all you hold sacred that you will never gamble again."

The Earl stared at her as if he could not believe what he had heard.

She went on:

"I am going to send you to the country to help Lord Flore repair his beautiful old Priory which is falling to pieces for want of attention."

The Earl, in a voice that did not sound like his own, said hesitatingly:

"Did you — say you would — pay my debts?"

"That is what I said," Malvina answered.

The Earl gave a little gulp and put his hand up to his face, and she knew he was fighting his tears.

"How can y-you — do th-that?" he stammered. "How c-can you — be so k-kind as to — s-save my l-life?"

"My father always helped people who came to him with their troubles," Malvina replied, "and, because he gave them confidence, nearly every one of them eventually paid him back."

"I will do that — I swear I will — do it," the Earl said, "if I have the — chance!"

He spoke through his tears, and his hands still covered his eyes.

Malvina rose and walked to her desk to give him time to compose himself.

"I am going to write to Lord Flore," she said,

"and as I think the sooner you leave London the better, I will send you to the country immediately, in one of my Phaetons."

She sat down and wrote quickly what she had intended to write anyway.

She told him that a representative from her Solicitor would be contacting him within a day or two.

Then she added:

I am sending you the Earl of Andover to start repairing your house. He will tell you himself why he has come. I am hoping you can help him, as Papa helped you.

She signed her name, and having sealed the letter, addressed it to Lord Flore.

While she had been writing, she had heard the Earl blowing his nose.

As she walked back to the sofa he rose to his feet and she could see that he had wiped his eyes.

He still, however, looked very young and rather pathetic, like a little boy who had got out of his depth in a whirlpool, and did not know how to swim.

"Now, here is the letter for Lord Flore," she said. "It will take you with my horses about three hours to reach him."

She handed the Earl the letter and went on:

"I want you now to give a detailed account to my Secretary of everything you owe. While you are doing so, I will arrange for you to have some-

66

thing to eat and drink."

"I do not — know what to say," the Earl said brokenly. "There are no words in which to — thank you."

"You can thank me by helping Lord Flore, who is also in trouble, but is one of those people who I am quite certain will get out of it."

"And you think — I can do the — same?" the Earl asked humbly.

Malvina smiled at him.

"I am quite sure you can. It may take a long time, but while you are struggling to find your feet, I am going to employ you. You will have a small allowance paid to you every month from which you can clothe yourself, and have enough money to tip those who serve you, and when it is necessary, buy your own food."

"I — cannot believe it!" the Earl exclaimed. "How can you — do all this when they call — you the 'Heartless Heiress' and the —"

He stopped.

"And what?" Malvina asked.

"I do not like to tell you," he said. "It is rude and unkind."

"I might as well know," she said, "and quite frankly, it does not worry me."

He looked away from her as if he were embarrassed before he said:

"They say — you are a — 'Man-Eating Tigress'!"

Malvina laughed.

"I rather like that!"

"I ought — not to have — told you."

"It does not worry me in the least," Malvina said, "but there is another thing you have to promise me."

"What is that?" he asked a little anxiously.

"It is that you tell no one except Lord Flore that I have paid your debts. If you let me down by confiding in even one of your friends, you can imagine how I would be besieged by an Army of impoverished Gentlemen asking me to fill their pockets."

"I swear I would do nothing that would hurt you," the Earl said, "when you have been so — unbelievably — kind."

He passed his hand over his eyes as he said:

"I think you are a Saint and I want to kneel at your feet and worship you, but instead I will vow to make myself — worthy of your — kindness."

He spoke so emotionally that Malvina was afraid he would cry again.

"I am quite sure you will do that," she replied lightly. "Now come along, and meet my Secretary, Mr. Cater, who was with my father, and I will send for my Phaeton, which I expect you will enjoy driving."

She saw the Earl's eyes light up, and he exclaimed:

"I do not believe this is happening! I am dreaming, and I know I shall wake up in my lodgings."

"You will wake up," Malvina said, "in what will be a somewhat dilapidated bed-room in

Flore Priory, and I think when you look at the walls of your room, and a great many others, you will complain that I have given you too daunting a task!"

"It could not be too much or too big for me!" the Earl boasted.

Malvina thought they had talked enough.

She wanted him to reach the Priory before nightfall, so she took him down the corridor to the Secretary's Room.

Mr. Cater was a middle-aged man whom her father had relied upon to keep his houses, his stables, and his estates in perfect order.

In the room were two comfortable armchairs which looked as if they were seldom sat in.

The rest of the furniture consisted mainly of tin boxes all labelled neatly with what they contained.

There were four boxes entitled: *MAULTON PARK.*

Malvina knew that everything inside them would be as neat and perfectly in order as the house and estate itself.

Mr. Cater rose when she entered and she smiled at him as she said:

"I have a task for you, Mr. Cater, and it is very important it should be done right away!"

She introduced the Earl and admired Mr. Cater's self-control when she said that she was paying all his debts.

"His Lordship will give you an account of every one of them," she said, "and while you are doing that I am going to order something for him to eat before he sets out for Flore Priory, where I am sending him."

Mr. Cater was writing down what she had said and she had the feeling that although he did not show any sign of it, he was moved.

"His Lordship is now in my employment," she went on, "and I wish you to give him a salary of sixty pounds a month."

This was quite a large sum, but Mr. Cater made a note without comment.

"As he will be working for me," Malvina continued, "I will provide his food; so will you send a letter to Mr. Doughty to tell him what I require done with the groom who accompanies His Lordship."

She turned to the Earl to explain:

"Mr. Doughty is the Manager in charge of Maulton Park estate."

The Earl did not answer; he merely stared at her.

She knew he was thinking once again that he was in a dream.

Malvina turned again to the Secretary.

"Tell Mr. Doughty he is to send to the Priory every day — eggs, chickens, cream, and butter, and when it is available, a leg of lamb."

She rose as she finished speaking and said:

"Now His Lordship will give you a list of what is to be paid."

She was moving towards the door when Mr. Cater remarked:

"You are so like your father, Miss Maulton! I could almost believe that he was speaking to me!"

Malvina laughed with delight.

Then she went into the hall to find a footman and told him to order a Phaeton drawn by two horses to be brought round immediately.

It was her father who had worked out a long time before exactly how long it would take to travel from London to Maulton Park.

He was continually trying to break his own record.

For people driving one horse it took four hours, and in a vehicle drawn by two horses it took three.

But when Magnamus Maulton travelled with four, drawing a Travelling Chariot which had been specially designed for lightness and speed, it took only two hours.

This, of course, depended very much on the season of the year.

In Winter, if the roads were covered with snow, it could take much longer because it was dangerous to go too fast.

As Malvina gave her orders she realised it had not rained for nearly a week.

The Earl could therefore reach the Priory in time for dinner.

Then she asked herself if there would be any dinner for him.

She had the feeling that Lord Flore might be insulted if she made him feel he was accepting her charity.

Then she told herself he was too practical to behave so foolishly over things that were of comparative unimportance.

She therefore went to the Kitchen herself.

She wanted to find out if the Chef had anything ready which would travel well.

It must, too, not require cooking when the Earl arrived at his destination.

The Chef was noted as one of the best in London.

He was also, Malvina thought, certainly one of the most expensive. He was delighted to see her.

When she told him what she wanted he produced a large pâté of chicken livers with truffles, which she thought looked delicious.

There was a whole salmon which had been cooked only the previous day and an ox-tongue which was warm.

"Have them put in the Phaeton," she said to the Chef, "and tell Newman to add a case of champagne."

She thought with a smile as she left the kitchen that she had forced Lord Flore to be obliged to her.

However much he might disapprove and dislike her as a woman, he could not refuse food for the Earl.

She went upstairs to tell her grandmother what was happening.

She thought that all she had to do now was to find him the heiress he required.

Then they could concentrate on making the race-course one of the best in the whole country.

After his meal, the Earl drove away in the Phaeton.

There was an expression on his face which made Malvina feel that she had given a small boy the largest present from the Christmas Tree.

"Do not forget to return first to your lodgings to pack your luggage," she reminded him.

"I would have forgotten," he admitted, "and when I am driving these horses I shall feel like Apollo traveling across the sky."

There was a note of rapture in his voice.

When he took her hand he squeezed it with such intensity that it hurt.

Once again he was being emotional, and Malvina said:

"Do not waste any time. You should be at Flore Priory by about six-thirty, and in case Lord Flore thinks you are presuming on him, your dinner is in the Phaeton."

The Earl gave her a look that told her without words he was worshipping her for her consideration.

Then he jumped into the high-seated Phaeton.

He took up the reins and the horses began to move off.

The Earl raised his hat.

Malvina saw that the groom accompanying him was an older man who would not allow him to take any risks, or drive the horses unnecessarily fast.

She watched the Phaeton out of sight, then went upstairs to her grandmother.

"What is going on?" the Dowager Countess asked. "I was told that the Earl of Andover was here. I presume he came to propose to you?"

"He did, but he is much too young to think of marrying," Malvina replied. "He has promised me he will go to the country, where I understand there is a great deal for him to do."

She did not say where he was going.

Her grandmother thought he was returning to his own house and estate.

"That was very sensible of you," the Dowager said. "It is bad for young men to hang about in London with nothing to do."

"I agree with you," Malvina said.

Then she went on:

"I cannot believe, Grandmama, that I am the only heiress in the whole country. There must be a great many other girls who have money?"

"Not as much as you have, my dear!" the Dowager replied.

"Who are the others?" Malvina asked.

She had, in fact, made enquiries last night of her partners at the Ball, and one of them had said:

"You are Heiress Number One! Now let me point out Number Two."

He glanced round the room.

Malvina saw the girl standing beside a chaperone, because no one had asked her to dance.

It was not surprising that she was a "Wall-flower."

She was exceedingly plain with dark hair, a long nose, and eyes that were too close together.

Malvina looked at her and asked:

"Is she really very rich?"

"She has thousands!" her partner replied. "And the poor girl will need it with a face like that!"

It flashed through Malvina's mind that it would serve Lord Flore right if she introduced him to the plain heiress.

She was quite certain that, as a wife, the heiress would be very compliant and do everything he asked of her.

Then she told herself it would be a jest at his expense, but it would hurt the girl.

She could not help being unattractive.

"Now you understand," her partner said, "why you are so much in demand! Even without a penny you would be completely and utterly desirable!"

"But I doubt whether you and a great many other men would be so eager to marry me!" Malvina replied.

"I should love to marry you!" her partner replied. "But I think you would be very uncomfortable living in a wooden hut or a cave, which is about all I can afford!"

Malvina laughed.

"At least you are truthful about it."

"It is about the only thing that costs nothing,"

he answered, and she laughed again.

Now, waiting for her grandmother to reply, she thought there must be other girls who were as pretty, or very nearly as pretty as herself!

"There was one girl at the Ball last night," her grandmother said, "whom we shall be meeting again this evening."

"Who is that?"

"Her name is Rosette Langley," her grandmother answered.

"Then the Ball we are attending to-night is being given for her?" Malvina exclaimed.

"It is," her grandmother replied, "and her aunt, who is bringing her out, is a very old friend of mine."

"I shall look forward to meeting her," Malvina said.

They arrived at the house in Park Lane where the Ball was being held.

Malvina looked with interest at the *débutante* as she was receiving her guests.

She was certainly very pretty in a somewhat fragile manner.

Malvina realised as she shook hands with her that she was shy.

Later in the evening one of her partners said:

"You are certainly very different, Miss Maulton, from our hostess!"

"In what way?" Malvina asked.

"Well, I find all *débutantes,* except for yourself, are a bore!" he replied. "In fact, I never speak to one if I can help it!"

"But you are here to-night," Malvina replied.

"A great number of my friends are present," he answered, "and until I met you, I preferred women who were married, sophisticated and, of course, very — amusing!"

He hesitated over the last word, and Malvina realised he had been about to say "desirable."

She knew the Gentleman in question had a reputation for breaking the hearts of a great number of lovely women.

As he had said himself, however, they were sophisticated and married.

He was not impoverished like the majority of her suitors.

But Malvina guessed that because he had a distinguished title, he was looking for a wife who would give him a son and heir.

It was also important that she should contribute blue blood or money to his family tree.

It was a time-honoured tradition in the Social World.

Malvina knew in some ways she was unique because she combined her mother's undoubted blue blood with her father's great fortune.

However distinguished her husband might be, he would not be able to look down on her.

Malvina was too observant not to realise that many of the women in the Ball-Room who were wearing dazzling jewels and expensive gowns did not look happy.

She made while she was dancing a few discreet

enquiries about them.

Some had been married for their money.

Others, because they were aristocrats, had their marriages arranged by their fathers so that blue blood could go to blue blood.

"I will marry *no one* unless I love him!" she decided.

She knew that so far, of all the men she had met, not one had caused a flicker in her heart.

"I want love . . . real love!" she told herself several times during the evening.

The partners with whom she was dancing were paying her extravagant compliments and holding her a little closer than was correct.

But she knew by the expression in their eyes that whatever their lips were saying, their minds were calculating how they would spend her millions.

"No! No! No!"

She thought that she said it over and over again until it came to her lips automatically.

Then, just before they were leaving, she found herself thinking of the race-course.

She remembered her obligation to Lord Flore.

She crossed the room to speak to Rosette Langley.

"I wonder," she said, "if you and your aunt would like to come down to Maulton Park on Friday and stay until Monday evening? The gardens look so lovely in the Spring, and there is no particularly important Ball taking place on Saturday night! Personally I would rather be riding."

78

Rosette gave her a shy smile.

"Thank you, how very kind of you to ask me," she said. "Are you quite sure I shall not be a bother?"

"I would love to have you!" Malvina replied. "And if your aunt is too busy to come, my grandmother, the Dowager Countess of Daresbury whom she knows well, will be chaperoning me, so you could come alone."

"That would be very nice," Rosette said.

"Then let me know to-morrow when you have talked to your aunt," Malvina said.

Her partner, who was a rather attractive young man, said as she turned away:

"If you are giving a house-party, may I come too?"

"Only if you stop proposing to me, and make yourself pleasant to everyone."

"I will do that," he said, "but I would like to look at your home, which I am told is magnificent!"

There was a note of greed in his voice which Malvina did not miss.

At the same time, he was quite amusing, and she knew, too, that he rode well.

"I will have a party of young people," she told herself, "and Lord Flore can have a close look at the Heiress."

Then she remembered that the Earl would be with him too.

"I suppose I should get a girl for him," she told herself. "I will find out from Grandmama if there is another pretty Heiress who would like to be a Countess."

Then she laughed at herself.

'I am becoming nothing but a match-maker!' she thought. 'But at least it is better than having to keep fighting myself free of men who want to drag me up the aisle!'

Before she went to sleep she found herself saying in the darkness:

"I want love . . . real love . . . and unless I find it, I will never marry!"

chapter four

The following day Malvina encountered Sir Mortimer.

It was at a luncheon-party which she and her grandmother attended.

It was not a very interesting one.

Also, she was slightly irritated to find that Sir Mortimer was seated next to her.

She had the idea that he had negotiated this in some way.

But he proceeded to make himself very pleasant, and she had no wish to quarrel.

When they had finished talking of various other things, he said:

"I wonder if your grandmother would either come, or permit me to take you to a party I want to give at Vauxhall Gardens on Saturday evening? There is a new Prima Donna from Italy who has astounded everybody with her magical voice."

"It is very kind of you," Malvina answered, "but we are going to the country."

"Again?" Sir Mortimer exclaimed sharply.

She knew he was thinking that Lord Flore

would take advantage of her presence.

She therefore said quickly:

"I am having a small house-party, all of whom enjoy riding as much as I do."

"Am I not invited?" Sir Mortimer enquired.

Malvina shook her head.

"Why not?"

"Do not be offended if I say that you are too old," she replied. "My Guest of Honour is Rosette Langley, whose aunt is a friend of my grandmother's, and I want her to have a happy time."

"I want to make *you* happy."

Sir Mortimer spoke insistently, but Malvina replied:

"I am sorry, but my party is now complete."

She saw the anger in his eyes and turned deliberately away to talk to the man on her other side.

Later, however, she had to turn back as Sir Mortimer said:

"I have something to say which I think you will find interesting."

"What is that?" Malvina enquired.

"A friend of mine, the Marquess of Ilminster, is putting some horses up for sale at Tattersalls next week. They are superb animals, and as I knew you would be interested, I asked him as a favour if you could see them first."

Malvina looked at him in surprise.

Then she understood that, if Sir Mortimer sold the horses for him before they reached the Sale room, he would earn a large commission.

At the same time, she could remember her father speaking of the Marquess of Ilminster.

On one occasion, there had been a close finish on the race-course between his horse and her father's.

"Are the horses really outstanding?" she asked.

"I am quite confident that if your father were alive, he would want to add them to his stables, and would certainly have appreciated the opportunity of seeing them before anybody else."

She hated to be under any sort of obligation to Sir Mortimer.

Yet Malvina thought it was too good a chance to miss.

"When may I see them?" she asked. "As you know, we are leaving for the country tomorrow."

"Quite a number have already reached London," Sir Mortimer replied, "and I arranged with His Lordship that we would inspect them as soon as luncheon is finished."

Malvina hesitated, and he added quickly:

"Of course, your grandmother can come too, to chaperon you."

They left the party as soon as it was polite to do so.

When Sir Mortimer got into her carriage, the Dowager looked at him in surprise.

"Sir Mortimer is taking me to see some magnificent horses belonging to the Marquess of Ilminster," Malvina said. "They are in his stables not far from here, and I know you, Grandmama, would also be interested in them."

The Dowager acquiesced, but when they actually reached the stables she said:

"If you do not mind, dear child, I think I will wait in the carriage. I am rather tired, and as you know, we have another party to-night."

"Yes, of course, Grandmama," Malvina agreed. "I will not be long."

They got out at the Mews, and Malvina found that His Lordship's stables were very much larger than she expected.

There were fifteen horses.

She saw at a glance that Sir Mortimer had not exaggerated when he had said how good they were.

A groom took them from one stall to another.

Finally she told Sir Mortimer that she would like to buy eight.

He told her the price, and she knew it was astronomical.

She was also quite certain that a large amount of the money would go into his own pocket.

But she knew that if they had gone to the Sale room, they might easily have reached the price Sir Mortimer was quoting.

Also, she would not have known that they were being sold.

She had been busy since she had come to London with buying clothes, and attending Balls and other parties.

She had therefore not ridden every day as she meant to do.

Also she had not visited Tattersalls as her father always did when there was a special Sale.

In fact, she thought a little guiltily, although Mr. Cater left the Sale Catalogues on her desk, she had not even glanced at them.

After a little hesitation she offered Sir Mortimer a considerably smaller sum than he was asking.

Then the bargaining began.

She had often heard her father negotiating a deal.

He had spoken in a quiet, calm voice.

It made the seller uncertain if he was or was not enthusiastic about the purchase.

She spoke in the same way.

As they discussed their business they moved out of the stables into the Mews.

Malvina was aware that her grandmother was watching them with surprise.

She and Sir Mortimer stood where they could not be overheard.

They talked for nearly a quarter-of-an-hour.

Finally he capitulated.

He accepted a sum which was far less than he had asked in the first place.

"You drive a hard deal, Malvina," he remarked.

"And you optimistically took me for a 'greenhorn'!" Malvina replied. "And, incidentally, my name is 'Miss Maulton'!"

"Nonsense!" Sir Mortimer exclaimed. "I have

no intention of being formal with you, and I suppose, as I have found you these horses, you would not like to change your mind and accept them as a wedding present?"

Malvina laughed.

If she did agree to anything so ridiculous, she would undoubtedly pay for the horses after they were married.

She went back into the stables to say she would send her own grooms to ride the horses down to the country.

She also tipped generously those who had shown them to her.

She thought as she walked back to the carriage that Sir Mortimer had certainly been well rewarded.

But he had given her the information in the first place.

She had not got a bargain.

On the other hand, she had horses which her father would have been proud to own.

They drove home, and as they did so her grandmother said:

"I do not like that man. There is something about him which is not right."

"I am well aware of that, Grandmama," Malvina said, "and he had the cheek to ask if he could join my house-party on Friday!"

"I hope you said no?" the Dowager asked quickly.

"I made it quite clear that he was too old," Malvina replied.

Her grandmother chuckled.

"He would not like that! He fancies himself as a dashing young Roué, but he is actually thirty-seven, and has pursued every heiress since he left School!"

Malvina laughed.

"I am doing my best to discourage him from pursuing me," she said.

"You are quite right to do so, dearest," her grandmother said firmly.

The next day they were to leave early in the morning for the country.

Malvina realised that she was excited.

She told herself it was because she was going home.

But she knew, if she was truthful, that it was because she wanted to hear more about the race-course.

She was also eager to find out if Lord Flore had accepted the Earl as she wanted him to do.

It must have been rather surprising to have a young man foisted upon him without any warning.

She wondered what he would say when the Earl told him she had paid his debts.

They arrived at Maulton Park in time for luncheon.

As soon as it was finished her grandmother went upstairs to lie down.

Malvina ran to the stables.

Hodgson was there, and she asked:

"Has Lord Flore been riding the horses?"

" 'E were 'ere s'marnin', Miss Malvina," Hodgson replied, " 'an 'e 'ad a young gent'man wi' 'im."

Malvina smiled.

"Saddle Dragonfly for me."

"Oi were sure tha's wot you'd want soon as ye arrive," Hodgson said, "an' Dragonfly be a-waitin's fer ye."

A stable lad brought Dragonfly out of his stall.

As Malvina patted him he nuzzled his nose against her.

She knew he was glad to see her.

"Who'll ye tak wi' ye, Miss?" Hodgson asked.

"No one," Malvina replied. "I am only going over to the Priory, and if I need an escort home, His Lordship will ride back with me."

"Then Oi won' worry 'bout ye," Hodgson said as he smiled.

"There has never been any reason why you should do so," Malvina retorted.

Hodgson lifted her onto the saddle.

She set off, knowing she would not have much time at the Priory before her house-party would begin to arrive at about tea-time.

She therefore hurried.

Not lingering in the wood as she usually did, she managed to reach the Priory in less than fifteen minutes.

There was no one to be seen.

She dismounted from Dragonfly, knotting the

reins very tightly so that they would not become loose.

Then she hurried up the steps.

There was no one in the Great Hall.

She walked along the passage, wondering where everybody could be.

As she opened a door into what Lord Flore had told her was known as the "Abbot's Room," she gave an exclamation.

Standing on a step-ladder in the middle of the room painting the ceiling was the Earl.

He certainly looked very different from how he had when she had last seen him.

He had no coat, his sleeves were rolled up, and there was no cravat round his neck.

He looked down, saw her, and exclaimed:

"Oh, Miss Maulton — it is you! How wonderful!"

He climbed down the ladder.

When she held out her hand he looked at his own rather ruefully.

It was covered in paint.

"I must not touch you," he said, "and you look very lovely!"

"What have you been doing?" she asked, looking up.

"I have almost finished the ceiling," he answered proudly, "then I am going to start on the walls."

"I told you there was a lot to do here!"

"But it is worth doing," he said. "I have never seen such a lovely house!"

"Where is Lord Flore?"

"He is in the next room," the Earl replied, "and he has something to show you."

"I will go and find him," Malvina answered.

"I will join you when I have finished this," the Earl said, "and washed my hands."

He climbed up the ladder again as if he were eager to get on with his task.

Malvina left him.

She opened the door of the next room and saw there was a large table in the centre of it.

Lord Flore was working on something which he had laid out on top of it.

He looked at her in surprise.

Then he said:

"Has London suddenly lost its sparkle, or were you just curious as to what I was getting up to?"

Because Malvina realised that was the truth, she laughed.

"You flatter yourself! I was in fact wondering how you had taken your unexpected guest."

"David is a nice boy," Lord Flore replied, "and I am working him very hard."

"I have just seen him, and I think he is enjoying himself," Malvina said.

She walked to the table as she spoke.

She realised that what Lord Flore was studying was a design for the race-course.

He had it spread out on the table.

He had marked the names of the various fields that it would cover on his land.

Then, as she looked closer, she saw that several fields on her estate were also included.

She did not have to ask the question.

Lord Flore answered it before she could speak.

"To make it as cheaply as possible," he said, "I am using land which will not have to be levelled, and which is eminently suitable either for steeple-chasing, or flat racing."

Malvina's eyes lit up, and he went on:

"Actually, I think we can manage both on the same course, although it will take a lot of planning."

Malvina clasped her hands together.

"But that is wonderful!" she said. "And it means that the racing can take place for at least nine months of the year."

"That is what I was thinking," Lord Flore agreed.

"How soon are you going to start?" Malvina asked breathlessly.

"As soon as you give me permission to include the fields on the Maulton estate."

"Include everything you want!" Malvina said excitedly. "After all, we are partners in this."

"You kept your promise?" Lord Flore asked sharply.

Malvina lifted her chin.

"I gave you my word!"

"All women talk too much."

"I think that can be said of a lot of men!" Malvina retorted.

"I suppose you are right," Lord Flore agreed. "At the same time, I do not want you talked about any more than you are already."

"Stop preaching at me," Malvina said, "and listen to what I have brought you."

"If it is a present," Lord Flore said quickly, "you can take it away. I have swallowed my pride in accepting food which is enough to keep an Army, and the champagne, which David enjoys, but I am not taking any more."

"It is not exactly a present," Malvina said demurely, "but I have brought you something you particularly wanted."

Lord Flore looked puzzled.

"An heiress!" Malvina said.

He stared at her.

"What are you talking about?"

"You told me you wanted an heiress who was soft, quiet, complacent, and amenable! Well, she is arriving at the Park this afternoon."

"Do not be so ridiculous!" Lord Flore said sharply. "I have no time for heiresses; I have a race-course to build!"

"You cannot be so ungrateful," Malvina said, "and if you do not come to dinner and bring His Lordship with you, I shall not allow either of you to ride the eight magnificent horses I have just bought from the Marquess of Ilminster!"

"I heard he was selling his horses," Lord Flore said, "but as I cannot afford a donkey, I was not particularly interested."

"They are going to be sold at Tattersalls to-morrow," Malvina said. "I have had a preview of them, and the best are arriving here to-morrow."

"How did you manage that?" Lord Flore asked.

Malvina hesitated a moment, then she told the truth.

"I am actually under an obligation to Sir Mortimer Smythe," she said. "He arranged with His Lordship that I should have the first choice."

"I suppose you know what he gets out of that?" Lord Flore remarked cynically.

"Quite a lot, I should imagine," Malvina said. "But it was a case of my taking the opportunity when it presented itself, or sending somebody else to bid for me to-morrow."

Lord Flore shrugged his shoulders.

"Well, you can afford it," he said, "and I have to admit that I shall look forward to seeing them."

"Then you will dine with me to-night and to-morrow night?" Malvina said.

He looked at her with a twinkle in his eye.

"Are you blackmailing me?" he asked.

"Of course, if I have to! But I am sure you will say you accept graciously and with pleasure."

"I accept," he said, "but all this poodle-faking is a waste of time."

"Not where you are concerned."

He looked at her.

"Are you serious? Have you really invited an heiress to stay with you? And are you seriously expecting me to be interested?"

93

There was so much incredulity in his voice that Malvina laughed.

"That is what you asked me to do."

"You know perfectly well that I was only speaking generally of the sort of woman I might marry."

"You will marry what I have found you!"

Lord Flore made an exasperated sound.

"I should have added that I have no wish to be married, and much prefer to be a free and unfettered bachelor."

There was silence, then Malvina said quietly:

"You have forgotten the Priory."

"I thought you sent me David to restore it."

"I can see he is doing his best," Malvina replied, "but you can hardly expect him to restore the whole place alone. It would take him a century!"

Lord Flore was silent for a moment. Then he said:

"Naturally, I was counting on our race-course to pay back the money you expended on it, and eventually — it may take a large number of years — make my home look as I wish it to do."

"Everything can be completed far more quickly if you marry," Malvina persisted.

There was a flash of anger in Lord Flore's eyes, and she had a feeling he was going to rage at her.

Then unexpectedly he said:

"Are you, or are you not interested in what I am planning for the race-course? We have a great number of things to discuss, and as my partner and, for the moment, the *Senior* partner, I am obliged to consult you."

"Of course that is what I want," Malvina agreed.

She was thinking as she walked nearer to the table that he had accentuated the word *"Senior."*

She knew perceptively that he was referring to her money, and inwardly she resented it.

It suddenly struck her that she had been rather foolish.

They had agreed that they should build a race-course together.

It was a mistake to involve him in what she knew now had been a light-hearted discussion about an heiress.

'I have been rather stupid about this,' she thought as she bent over the plan.

He had a reason for telling her what sort of wife he wished to acquire.

It was to reassure her that she had no chance of ever qualifying for the position.

She had taken him seriously.

Now Rosette Langley would be arriving at about five o'clock.

Malvina was sure her supposition was right, especially as Lord Flore spoke to her in what she thought was a hard, businesslike tone.

He began to explain exactly what he had planned.

"The stands will be here," he was saying, pointing with a pencil, "the Bookies can congregate here by the winning-post, and the Jockey Club will, of course, be opposite it."

"It looks as if you have thought of everything," Malvina said.

"There will be two entrances to the course," Lord Flore went on, "one over my land and one over yours. We will have to provide stabling and a number of other things I have not yet drawn in."

"It looks very exciting already," Malvina said, "and I hope my Solicitor has been in touch with you, as he promised."

"His representative arrived yesterday," Lord Flore replied. "An intelligent man. He agreed to everything I suggested."

"What did you suggest?" Malvina asked.

"I stated that once the race-course is built and in operation, every penny it accrues will be credited to you until my share of the expenditure is entirely paid off."

"That is absurd!" Malvina expostulated. "You will have a great number of expenses, and because your house is on the course, you know as well as I do that a number of people will expect to stay with you."

She had the idea that Lord Flore had not thought of that.

Then he said harshly:

"Then they will be disappointed! We are near enough to London for them to come for the day, and return once the racing is over."

"I am sure the majority will do that," Malvina agreed. "At the same time, because you are someone of consequence, and I am the same, I think you will find that accommodation in both our houses will be constantly in demand."

"This is not meant just to be a social amusement," Lord Flore said. "It is a money-making concern."

"Well, I intend to enjoy it," Malvina said, "and if you are going to be disagreeable about everything, and argue over every penny that is expended, it is going to be a constant battle between us."

He looked at her, she thought, in a hostile manner as he said:

"You are determined to have your own way."

"I have every intention of doing so!"

Their eyes met, and she felt as if they crossed swords.

"Dammit!" Lord Flore swore angrily. "This is my idea, and I wish I could do it without you!"

"I am well aware of that," Malvina said coldly. "However, you cannot, so unless you marry an heiress you will have to put up with me!"

As she finished speaking she knew Lord Flore was longing to say he would find himself another partner.

Then because she thought it was a mistake to keep quarrelling, she said in a more conciliatory tone:

"Do stop being so cross and hating me."

He did not answer, and she went on:

"I expect your 'apprentice' has told you what my new name is in the Clubs, and it is what you are thinking at the moment!"

" 'A man-eating tigress'?" Lord Flore asked. "It is an insult, and actually it is not true."

"You think it untrue?" Malvina enquired in surprise.

"I think you are infuriating, exasperating, and much too puffed up with your own importance," Lord Flore said. "At the same time, you were kind to David Andover, and you saved the young man from taking his own life."

His voice softened as he spoke, and Malvina blushed.

"What else could I do?" she murmured. "And I remembered that you had said that Papa helped you."

"I am glad I had some part in your decision," Lord Flore said, "but I am not a very good example of your father's generosity."

"At least you were not running away from your problems," Malvina said quickly.

"I think my biggest problem at the moment," Lord Flore said surprisingly, "is to prevent you from having your name bandied about as if you were a second-rate chorus girl!"

"I cannot see why that should concern you!" Malvina snapped.

Then, as he was silent, she added:

"I suppose you are thinking that if we are partners, it might make your reputation worse than it is already."

"Yes, that is what I was thinking," Lord Flore agreed.

She thought the way he spoke, a little too quickly, was insincere.

Then he said:

"Well, as you are here for the next two days, I would like you to ride with me over the fields where the race-course will be, and see if there is anything I have forgotten."

Malvina's eyes lit up.

"I would love to do that!"

"Then you will have to come alone," he said, "and remember — not a word to anybody who is staying in your house."

"No, of course not," she agreed. "But you will have to tell David Andover to keep quiet."

"He is so grateful for what you have done for him, he would never do anything that might hurt you in any way," Lord Flore replied.

"Are you riding to-morrow morning?" Malvina asked.

"If you will allow me to do so."

"The person who will be grateful to you is Hodgson," Malvina said. "Do not forget, he has eight extra horses arriving to-morrow, and will not have time to take on any more grooms."

"Then, of course, David and I will both visit the stable," Lord Flore replied.

"I will join you at six-thirty to-morrow morning," Malvina said.

"I shall be waiting for you," Lord Flore replied, "but perhaps David had better have his 'Beauty Sleep.'"

It struck Malvina that she would much rather be alone with him.

She took another look at the plan for the race-course.

Then she said:

"I suppose I should be getting back."

At that moment the Earl came into the room.

He had washed his hands, put on a coat, and had a loose scarf round his neck.

"You are not leaving?" he asked in consternation.

"I have to," Malvina said, "because I have a lot of charming people coming to stay, and you and Lord Flore are to meet them at dinner."

"Are we dining with you?" the Earl asked, and his eyes lit up. "That will be fun!"

"I am sure you will think so," Malvina replied. "I have some very beautiful young ladies staying with me, and a number of men who I am sure you will know."

She thought the Earl looked apprehensive, and added:

"If they are curious, just say that you are staying with Lord Flore, whom you have known for a long time."

"They may think it strange that I am not in London," the Earl suggested tentatively.

"If you are questioned further, just be silent and let them think you are running away from your difficulties. And you must not let them be too inquisitive."

"No, of course not," the Earl agreed.

The two men walked beside Malvina back through the Great Hall.

"One day," she said, "you must give a dinner-party here. I feel it would be very impressive, and very romantic."

"The ghosts of the monks might disapprove!" Lord Flore remarked.

"Nonsense!" Malvina retorted. "They would give us their blessing."

"That is what they will certainly give to you," the Earl said in a low voice, "just as you have blessed me!"

Malvina looked away from the gratitude in his eyes.

"Come and meet Dragonfly," she said. "However much you and Lord Flore may rave over the new horses I have just bought, Dragonfly takes first place in my heart."

She thought any of the men who flattered her in London would have said:

"Just as you take first place in mine!"

But the Earl was patting Dragonfly.

She knew that he was not thinking of her as an attractive woman, but as a Saint who had saved him from destruction.

Lord Flore was aware of what she was thinking.

She saw his eyes twinkling, and there was a mocking smile on his lips.

"We will brush up our clothes and our compliments this evening," he promised.

She knew then that she had been correct in knowing he was reading her thoughts.

Then, before the Earl could do so, Lord Flore lifted her into the saddle.

He arranged her riding skirt over the stirrup.

"I told you not to ride alone," he said, "but it is too late now for me to saddle one of my poor old nags to accompany you."

"I told Hodgson that was what you would do," Malvina replied.

"As I disapprove of you riding alone," Lord Flore replied, "I shall tell Hodgson, when you are in residence, to leave one of your horses in my stable."

He spoke firmly, as if he would brook no argument.

If he expected her to protest, he was disappointed.

Instead, she said:

"Stop trying to tell me what I shall do and what I shall not do. It is just like listening to a fussy Schoolteacher!"

She took up Dragonfly's reins.

She rode off before Lord Flore could think of a rejoinder.

She went back through the wood, and when she came in sight of the house, she saw there was a carriage outside the door.

Her guests were already arriving.

She suddenly found herself resenting how much time she would have to spend with them.

Instead, she might be at the Priory.

She wanted to go on discussing the racecourse with Lord Flore.

He might think he had remembered everything.

She was, however, determined to make her contribution to the plan by finding something he had overlooked.

'There is so much I want to talk to him about,' she thought.

Then she remembered she would see him again at dinner.

Although they could not talk about the race-course, it was fun to know that they shared a secret.

She knew it would be a juicy morsel of gossip once London Society got to hear of it.

She could imagine only too well what the Bucks in the Clubs would think.

It was that Lord Flore had "stolen a march" on them.

They would be convinced she had agreed to marry him.

The women would aver spitefully, because they were jealous, that he was marrying her only for her money.

At least they could not say that she was marrying him for his title.

She had refused a Duke.

They would have much pleasure in predicting she would be unhappy.

Lord Flore was undoubtedly a Rake and a Rogue.

As she thought it over she could understand that he was quite right in saying he did not want her talked about.

Of course it was degrading that her name should occur so frequently in the Betting Book at Whites Club.

'I ought to have been a boy,' she thought.

She knew that her father always regretted he had not had a son.

Had she been a boy, someone would undoubtedly have loved her for herself.

'I suppose now that will never happen,' she thought dismally.

An idea suddenly struck her.

When she did finally marry, she would never be quite certain of her husband.

Would he have asked her to be his wife if she had nothing but her looks and herself to give him?

It was an unhappy thought.

She tried to dismiss it from her mind.

She walked into the Drawing-Room to find Rosette Langley, her mother, and several gentlemen waiting to greet her.

Later that evening, Malvina looked down the Dining-Room table.

She thought she could be very proud of what was her first party at Maulton Park.

Her grandmother and Lady Langley were glittering.

They had tiaras on their heads and a number of sparkling jewels round their necks and wrists.

The girls, like Rosette, wore no jewellery apart from a string of small pearls.

But there were flowers in their hair and pinned to their gowns.

It made them look like flowers themselves.

Malvina wanted her guests to enjoy themselves.

So in the same way her mother would have done, she paid no attention to their social position.

She placed each person where she thought they would have the most fun.

She therefore had been rather clever in not placing Rosette beside Lord Flore.

She thought she might find him rather overpowering.

Instead, he was almost opposite her.

He could then look at her and, Malvina thought, appreciate her beauty.

Instead, she put David Andover on one side of Rosette, while a man who was about the same age was on the other.

Lord Flore was on Malvina's right.

On his other side was a young lady of twenty who was very talkative, and rather flirtatious.

She had no fortune.

She was, in fact, trying to marry another man in the party.

He was the elder son of the Marquess of Frome, a favourite with all the ambitious mothers.

Malvina had danced with him several times.

She thought he was rather spoiled and conceited.

He had made up his mind already that he would not marry until he was very much older.

He enjoyed riding, and had a pack of his own fox-hounds.

She was considering joining in the Winter.

The dinner-party was young and good-looking.

So far as the men were concerned, they were exceedingly smart.

Their cravats were well-tied, and the points of their collars were high above their chins.

They were all sporting the long black drain-pipe trousers as an alternative to silk stockings and knee-breeches.

These had been invented by the King when he was Prince Regent.

Mr. Cater had carried out every suggestion with his usual perfection that Malvina had put to him.

When dinner was over there was a small Orchestra to play in one of the rooms.

To-morrow night there would be a bigger one in the Ball-Room.

At such short notice, it was impossible to have a very large party.

But by sending grooms in every direction, Malvina already had fifty acceptances for to-morrow.

"We must have a Cotillion," she had told Mr. Cater, "with lots of pretty presents for the ladies."

He made a note and she went on:

"The King so enjoyed his visit to Scotland that now quite a number of people like dancing the Reels."

Mr. Cater had therefore arranged for a Piper to play during the evening.

'To-night, we must all go to bed early,' she thought, 'otherwise I shall be tired when I have to meet Lord Flore at half-past-six.'

"What are you thinking about?" he asked.

She lowered her voice:

"To-morrow morning."

"If you are asleep, I shall understand."

"I was just thinking we should all go to bed early."

Then because she was curious she asked in a low voice:

"What do you think of her?"

Lord Flore made no pretence of not understanding.

He looked across the table to where Rosette was listening wide-eyed to something David was saying to her.

She was, however, Malvina thought, saying very little herself.

Lord Flore did not answer, and she said:

"She is very pretty!"

"Unfledged and just out of the egg!" he replied.

"That is what you wanted."

"I know, but I am just wondering what we would talk about in the long Winter evenings."

"You would talk, and she would listen!" Malvina said mockingly. "And she occasionally would interrupt your discourse by saying how clever and wonderful you are!"

"Of course you are right!" Lord Flore agreed. "And it is the correct ending to a romantic novel."

He paused before he looked at her and said sarcastically:

"It will be interesting to see how you end your own story."

"Are you determined it will not be romantic?" Malvina asked.

She remembered as she spoke how she had already decided it would be difficult to believe a man would marry her for herself.

Instead of saying even if it was untrue that because she was so beautiful any man she took as a husband would love her desperately, Lord Flore said:

"I think you will find it very difficult to separate the chaff from the grain, and you are too young to have the responsibility."

Malvina stiffened.

"What you are saying," she said, "is that I am too stupid not to know when a man is making up to me because he wants what I possess."

"You think you are very clever," Lord Flore said, "but women are easily deceived. You have only to read the History Books and the newspapers to be aware of that!"

"Then I hope I will prove to be the exception!" Malvina said coldly. "And we are not concerned at the moment with my affairs, but with yours."

"You are so kind to me," he said, "that I really feel quite embarrassed."

He was speaking sarcastically.

Once again there was that mocking look in his eyes, and a twist to his lips that she disliked.

She longed to make him realise how much she resented the way he tried to interfere in her life.

But it was now time for the ladies to leave the gentlemen to their port.

She rose to her feet.

Her grandmother and Lady Langley walked towards the door.

As she followed them, Rosette moved to her side and slipped her hand into hers.

"It is so exciting being here!" she said. "Thank you . . . thank you so much for asking me!"

As they walked towards the door, Malvina decided the girl was very sweet.

Whatever Lord Flore might say, she was sure she would suit him admirably.

chapter five

Malvina thought the dance was being a great success.

The Cotillion had gone off exactly as she had hoped.

Rosette had received more presents and flowers than any of the other girls.

At the same time, no one had been allowed to be a "Wallflower."

Malvina was sitting down for a moment, watching her guess dancing.

Lord Flore joined her.

As he did so, Rosette and the Earl danced by, both looking exceedingly attractive.

Rosette, in a pink evening-gown, was like a rose just coming into bloom.

"She is very pretty," Malvina remarked.

Lord Flore followed the direction of her eyes and replied:

"I agree with you, but I am at the moment feeling somewhat old."

Malvina laughed.

"Actually, that is something I am feeling myself."

He did not say anything, and she went on:

"I have travelled so much with Papa and met so many people from distant lands that girls of my own age seem like my daughters rather than my contemporaries!"

"Now you are really frightening me!" Lord Flore said. "We will have to find you an ancient husband on sticks so that he will satisfy your brain."

Malvina knew he was teasing her, and laughed.

"We are both being very pompous," she said. "I keep thinking about the race-course, and wishing we could get on with it."

"Once we start, it will not take very long," Lord Flore replied.

"Then let us start at once," Malvina said eagerly, "otherwise we shall miss the Racing Season this year and have to wait until the Spring."

"We will have to be prepared for that," he said. "We may run into a number of unexpected snags before we can actually open the gates to the Public."

"I think you are being too slow and too cautious," Malvina said provocatively.

She waited for his reply.

Before he could speak one of the Ladies who had come from a neighbouring house stood in front of her.

She was, Malvina thought, very attractive in a sophisticated manner.

She had dark hair in which glittered an emerald tiara.

Her eyes seemed to reflect her jewels and, as she put out both of her hands to Lord Flore, in a somewhat affected manner she said:

"You are neglecting me, Shelton, and when I heard you would be here to-night, I was so looking forward to seeing you."

Lord Flore rose to his feet, saying:

"I had no idea, Charlotte, that you were back in England."

"I came home a month ago," the Lady replied, "and I expected to find you in London."

"I live here in the country," Lord Flore explained.

"Does it matter where it is as long as we have found each other again?"

She looked up at him. Her eyes and her whole poise were very eloquent.

Malvina, who had been staring at her spellbound, rose and walked away.

She knew she was not wanted.

If this was the sort of woman Lord Flore admired, then she had wasted her time in trying to find him a young heiress.

On her travels with her father she had encountered, in India and many other parts of the world, beautiful women exactly like "Charlotte."

They had made it very clear that any attractive man was fair game.

Now she could recall quite a number of women who had spoken to her father in exactly the same manner.

They had made it clear that they were his for the taking.

While her mother had been alive, as far as he was concerned, no other woman existed.

After her death Malvina realised that he compared every woman he met, however beautiful she might be, with the wife he had lost.

He was therefore not interested.

Now she was sure that Lord Flore had enjoyed an *affaire de coeur* with Charlotte who had "found him again."

She thought angrily this might interfere with his work on the race-course.

A little later she looked around the Ball-Room.

Neither Lord Flore nor Charlotte were anywhere to be seen.

She supposed they had found a place where they could be alone.

Perhaps Lord Flore was complimenting her and speaking to her of love.

Because she was wearing a tiara, it was obvious she was a married woman.

In which case he was wasting his time.

Malvina thought it over.

She knew she was resenting his preoccupation with anyone who could not help him in his struggle to restore his house and his estate.

She found herself still thinking of this when the dancing came to an end.

The guests from the other houses in the neighbourhood began to leave.

Charlotte came up to her to say:

"Thank you, Miss Maulton, for a lovely evening which I have enjoyed immensely!"

She looked, as she spoke, to where Lord Flore was waiting for the Earl.

Without saying any more to Malvina, she moved towards him, saying:

"Shelton dearest, you will not forget your promise, and I shall be waiting eagerly to hear from you."

"I will not forget, Charlotte, and good-night!" Lord Flore replied, kissing her hand.

The party left.

Lord Flore with some difficulty persuaded the Earl that it was time to go.

He was talking to Rosette, and she was laughing.

She looked very pretty as she did so.

Malvina thought Lord Flore must be extremely stupid if he preferred "Charlotte" to Rosette and her fortune.

"It has been a wonderful evening, wonderful!" the Earl exclaimed effusively. "And please bring some of the party over to the Priory to-morrow. I want to show Rosette the work I have been doing."

Malvina smiled.

"I hope," she said to Lord Flore, who was standing beside him, "that you are feeling hospitable."

"David and I will be delighted to see you before or after luncheon," he said.

Malvina laughed.

She knew by now there was nobody to cook for them at the Priory, with the exception of one very old woman who was the Butler's wife.

She had been there for over fifty years.

She did her best, but Malvina was sure she would not be able to cope with more than the two men.

"I expect," she answered, "that as to-morrow is Sunday, Grandmama will want to go to Church, so we had better come after luncheon."

"I shall look forward to seeing you," Lord Flore said, "and thank you for a delicious dinner."

He spoke formally.

Malvina wondered if he had really enjoyed himself.

As Malvina walked upstairs to bed, Rosette said:

"I have heard so much about the Priory and how beautiful it is that I would really like to visit it."

"That is what you shall do," Malvina said, "but I expect most of the men will prefer to go for a long ride."

As they reached Rosette's room she kissed Malvina affectionately.

"It was a lovely evening," she said. "I have never enjoyed myself so much."

There was no doubt she was completely sincere.

When Malvina was alone in her own bedroom, she wished she could say the same.

She could not help feeling that something was missing.

She was not quite certain what it was.

At least Rosette, the Earl, and, of course, the Lady called "Charlotte," had enjoyed themselves.

She found herself thinking of emeralds and green eyes long after she ought to have been asleep.

The following morning everybody was very late for breakfast.

None of the girls had come downstairs when Malvina drove with her grandmother and Lady Langley to Church.

When they arrived back at the house, Malvina went into the Drawing-Room.

She found to her astonishment that Sir Mortimer Smythe was there.

She had gone into the room alone, as her grandmother and Lady Langley went upstairs.

"Why are you here?" she asked sharply.

"I had to see you," he replied, "and it is very important!"

He spoke in a way that made her look at him apprehensively.

It flashed through her mind that perhaps he had found out that she had paid the Earl's debts, or else in some unaccountable manner he was aware that she and Lord Flore were about to build a race-course.

In the same tone he said:

"We shall be interrupted if I tell you about it here. Take me somewhere where your friends will not join us."

Malvina opened the door at the end of the Drawing-Room.

It led into a smaller room which was not often used.

It was, however, very attractively decorated.

Like all the rooms in the Hall, there was a profusion of flowers which scented the air.

As Sir Mortimer followed her and shut the door behind her, she asked sharply:

"What is all this about? I cannot think why you should have followed me to the country."

"I followed you because I have something to tell you which I know you will find not only interesting, but exciting!"

"What is it?" Malvina asked.

She did not sit down, but stood in front of the fireplace.

Sir Mortimer, however, seated himself on the sofa and said:

"Come and sit next to me. We do not want to be overheard."

"I cannot think what all this is about!" Malvina answered crossly.

"Well, first let me tell you," he said, "that your grooms have collected six of the horses you bought from the Marquess, and I imagine they arrived yesterday evening."

Malvina felt guilty.

She had been so busy with the party and the

dance, she had omitted to enquire if the horses had come home.

It was then she realised what Sir Mortimer had just said.

"You said *six!* What about the other two?" she asked.

"That is what I am going to tell you," he said. "I had them kept in London."

"*You* had them kept in London?" Malvina repeated. "But why should you interfere with what belongs to me?"

"I had a very good reason for doing so," he replied, "and I know it is something that will thrill you!"

Malvina stared at him.

He might have done her a service in telling her about such good horses.

At the same time, he had no right to alter her arrangements.

"The two horses I told the Marquess's Head Groom to keep back," he said, "are the best His Lordship has ever driven."

He paused, and as Malvina did not speak, he went on:

"I therefore believe that if you race them to-morrow against Lady Laker's, you will not only win a resounding victory, but also contribute a thousand guineas to a very worthy cause."

"I do not know what you are talking about!" Malvina said.

"It is quite simple," Sir Mortimer said. "A friend of mine has offered one-thousand guineas as a prize to anyone who can beat Lady Laker driving his horses in a Phaeton which he has just had built."

Malvina opened her lips to speak, but Sir Mortimer went on:

"Another thousand guineas will go to the Orphanage that Sir Hector intends to endow in London for the children who are abandoned heartlessly in the slums, where they usually die of neglect or starvation."

Sir Mortimer put out his hand pleadingly towards Malvina as he said:

"I know no one except yourself who can drive well enough to beat Lady Laker or have the right horses with which to do so."

"How do you know I drive so well?" Malvina snapped.

Sir Mortimer smiled.

"Do you imagine that everything about you is not known? You ride superbly, you drive well, you speak a number of foreign languages, besides being overwhelmingly beautiful!"

Because the way he spoke made her feel embarrassed, Malvina said:

"How could I possibly take part in a race of that sort?"

Sir Mortimer sighed.

"If you will not do so, then Sir Hector, who is a difficult man, will keep his money in his pocket and, although Lady Laker may get some of it, the Orphanage will be forgotten."

Malvina hesitated.

"There must be somebody else besides me."

"I know of no one who can drive as well as you or who has the right horses," Sir Mortimer said simply.

He spoke in a manner which made Malvina think he was in fact telling the truth.

Because she felt reluctant to do what he asked and because she disliked him, she said:

"If I lend you my horses, surely you can find somebody else to drive them?"

"I suppose there must be women drivers who are nearly as good as you," he replied, "but it would take time to find them; and are you prepared to risk your horses, which you know are superlative, to a complete stranger?"

Malvina sighed.

"The whole thing seems very strange," she said, "and actually, Grandmama and I are not leaving for London until after luncheon."

"If you leave early to-morrow morning," Sir Mortimer exclaimed, "it will not take you much more than two hours to reach London. The race begins at twelve o'clock, and you can easily be in Berkeley Square by five o'clock."

"Where does the race take place?" Malvina asked.

She knew by the expression on Sir Mortimer's face that he thought she had acceded to his suggestion.

It annoyed her, but she was finding it hard to refuse.

"What has been planned," Sir Mortimer said,

"is that you and Lady Laker start in the Regents Park and drive to a house which is just the other side of Potters Bar. It will take less than an hour. You will have luncheon there, accept the prize money, then return to London."

There was a triumphant note in his voice as he finished.

"And do you really mean," Malvina asked, "that Sir Hector will not give the money to the Orphanage if I do not accept the challenge?"

"He will have to cancel the arrangements that have been made for to-morrow," Sir Mortimer replied, "and although another race might be arranged later, he is one of those men who can be wildly enthusiastic about something to-day and show no interest in exactly the same thing to-morrow."

Malvina understood exactly what he was saying.

There was silence for quite a long time before she said:

"Well . . . I suppose . . . I could do . . . it."

"I knew you would be sporting about it," Sir Mortimer answered, "and when I told Sir Hector I was going to ask you to challenge Lady Laker's assertion that no one could beat her, he said:

" 'If she is Magnamus Maulton's daughter, then it will certainly be a tip-top race!' "

Malvina made up her mind.

"Very well," she said, "I will race my two horses, but I am sure Grandmama will not approve."

"Then why upset her?" Sir Mortimer asked.

"Are you suggesting I do not tell her?"

"Tell her at tea-time," he said. "I admire your grandmother, but I am sure it would be a great mistake for her to worry all day in case you had an accident or got over-tired. Now, what you must do is this . . ."

He rose to his feet as if he found it easier to talk when he was standing up.

"I will drive you to London," he began, "and we will leave about seven-thirty, when your grandmother will not even have been called. We will leave her a note saying you have an unexpected engagement, but will join her in Berkeley Square at tea-time."

He made a gesture with his hands, then he said:

"She will therefore not worry about you, and you must not tell anyone else about the race until it is all over."

"I . . . I suppose I could . . . do that," Malvina murmured.

"You know how older women fuss, especially when it is over someone as precious as you are!" Sir Mortimer said. "My advice is, do what you want, and talk about it afterwards."

Malvina thought it was the sort of thing he would say.

Aloud she replied:

"I dislike keeping things secret from Grandmama."

Even as she spoke she knew she was being hypocritical.

She had not told the Dowager Countess about the plan for the race-course.

Finally, because she felt guilty, she said:

"All right, Sir Mortimer, I will do what you want, and I suppose now that you are here and wish to leave with me to-morrow, you want to stay the night?"

"I came by Post Chaise," he said, "and I should find it very uncomfortable to have to return to London to-night and be back again so early in the morning."

Unexpectedly Malvina laughed.

"I see exactly the way your brain is working," she said, "and whether I like it or not, you have joined my house-party!"

"You must forgive me if I seem to have intruded," Sir Mortimer said humbly, "but I do want you to win that race."

"It will be very ignominious if I fail."

Malvina rose to her feet, saying as she did so:

"I suppose really I ought to bring a maid with me if I am travelling alone with you."

"You must do what you want," Sir Mortimer replied, "but if we are using your fast Phaeton, which I think is even lighter than Lady Laker's, we shall be very cramped."

There was no doubt that this was true.

Malvina was aware that they would both be uncomfortable if there were a third person with them.

Then she told herself that she was fussing unnecessarily.

She was going straight to her own house in London.

The Housekeeper and Mr. Cater would be adequate chaperons.

During the drive there would be a groom behind them.

She could tell Hodgson to send one of the older grooms who had known her for years.

'Sir Mortimer can hardly try any of his tricks in the circumstances,' she thought.

She went upstairs to take off her bonnet.

When she came down she found Sir Mortimer being very effusive to her grandmother and to Lady Langley.

She realised he could be charming when it suited him.

Her grandmother had said she did not like him.

But it was difficult not to respond to the complimentary things he was saying.

He concentrated on the two elder ladies the whole afternoon.

When they visited the Priory he did not make any unpleasant remarks about Lord Flore.

In fact, he went out of his way to praise the building.

Malvina was aware, however, that Lord Flore was surprised to see him.

But, as her grandmother was eager to see the Priory itself, the two men had little to say to each other.

They walked through what had once been

magnificent rooms and reached the Chapel.

Malvina was suddenly aware that the Earl and Rosette were no longer with them.

She supposed the Earl was showing her the work he was doing in the Abbot's Room.

They had therefore been left behind.

When they were in the Picture Gallery Lady Langley said:

"Where is Rosette? She is so fond of pictures that I am sure she would want to see these."

"Shall I go and find her?" Malvina offered. "It is easy to get lost in such a large building."

Lady Langley was not listening.

Lord Flore was showing her an Italian picture which needed restoring although it still contained some of its original beauty.

There was no chance of Malvina having a word alone with him.

When they went downstairs into the Great Hall, they found Rosette and the Earl waiting for them.

"I am sorry, Aunt, that I lost you," Rosette said, "but I felt a little tired after dancing so late last night."

"I am sure you can come and see the rest of the house another time," Lady Langley answered, "but I am sorry you missed the Picture Gallery."

"I do hope you will let me come another day," Rosette said to Lord Flore.

"You are welcome anytime!" he replied with a smile.

Malvina thought he was certainly being very pleasant.

When they all got back into the carriage which had brought them to the Priory, Lady Langley said:

"It is pathetic to see that lovely old house in such a terrible state! Why do they not restore some of the pictures and spend some money on repairs?"

"Because Lord Flore behaved so badly," the Dowager replied, "I expect his father would have made sure that everything was entailed."

"Yes, of course," Lady Langley said. "I had forgotten. He really did behave abominably."

"What did he do?" Rosette asked.

She looked so young and so pretty asking the question.

There was a moment's embarrassed silence.

Then Sir Mortimer made a joke about something quite different which made them laugh.

Malvina actually felt grateful to him.

Nevertheless, when she came downstairs at seven-thirty the following morning she felt guilty.

Her grandmother would certainly disapprove of her going up to London with Sir Mortimer to drive in a race.

Also she thought Lord Flore would be even more vehement about it.

It was only when she was dressing that she realised it would undoubtedly make her more talked about than she was already.

She could imagine what he would say about that!

'It is not his business!' she thought.

126

At the same time, she was his partner.

She had no wish to make him any more antagonistic about her behaviour than he was already.

Anyway, it was too late to change her mind now.

If she won the thousand guineas from Sir Hector and added another thousand of her own money, she would actually be doing a good deed.

Even Lord Flore could not say that was wrong.

She thought, however, when she had stepped into the Phaeton that was waiting for her in the stable-yard, there was a gleam in Sir Mortimer's eyes which she disliked.

She also thought that Hodgson looked reproachful as he said:

"Oi've gi' ye two o' our fastest pair, Miss Malvina, an' Oi 'opes the gent'man'll not spring 'em!"

"I am sure he will not, Hodgson," Malvina said consolingly.

They were just out of ear-shot of Sir Mortimer.

At the same time, because Hodgson was nervous, she was nervous too.

She knew it was a mistake to drive herself when she had to drive in a race a little later on.

She suddenly wished that she had not given in to Sir Mortimer.

She could have contributed towards the Orphanage without taking part in the race.

It was something she had not thought of until,

in the night, she had decided she would double the prize money.

The horses, which were fresh, were on the move.

Sir Mortimer seemed to handle the reins in an experienced manner.

In fact, Malvina found he did drive quite well, although not as well as her father and not as well as Lord Flore.

But he did reach London in two-and-a-half hours, longer than she generally took.

But it still gave her plenty of time to have something to eat and for the Marquess of Ilminster's horses to be put between the shafts.

They had been brought to her stables from the Marquess's.

When she saw them waiting for her outside the front-door, she knew she was very lucky to be the possessor of anything so superb.

As she set off for the Regents Park, sitting in the driver's seat, she began to feel rather excited.

"Why is Lady Laker considered to be such a skilful driver?" she asked Sir Mortimer.

"She is older than you are," he replied, "and has had a lot of experience."

"I shall be interested to meet her," Malvina said. "Will Sir Hector be waiting for us in the Regents Park?"

"He may be, but I think you will find he has gone ahead to greet you when you get to the house."

"Is it his?"

"No, actually it belongs to a friend of mine," Sir Mortimer replied. "He is in the North at the moment, but he always allows me to use his house when it suits me."

"That is nice for you," Malvina remarked.

"I promise you you shall have a very good luncheon," Sir Mortimer replied.

They reached the Regents Park.

Malvina was perturbed to find that a crowd of people was gathered there.

One look at Lady Laker's horses and the Phaeton she was driving told Malvina that it was not going to be an easy victory.

Lady Laker herself was a surprise.

She must, Malvina thought, be twenty-seven or twenty-eight years of age.

She was very attractive in a somewhat strange manner.

She was painted and powdered as if she were giving a performance in a Play House.

Her red hair, which was quite obviously not natural, was accentuated by a bonnet trimmed with a large amount of feathers.

It matched the brilliant green driving-coat she wore which was trimmed with dozens of buttons and white braid.

Lady Laker greeted Sir Mortimer with a cry of delight and kissed him on both cheeks.

Then, as he introduced her to Malvina, she said:

"Are you really my opponent? You look too young to be driving anything but a pony-carriage."

Malvina was not certain whether it was a compliment or not.

She smiled and said:

"I see you have two magnificent horses!"

" 'His Nibs' has seen to that!" Lady Laker replied. "He hopes to make a lot of money out of this race."

Malvina was surprised.

Then a number of smartly dressed gentlemen surged round them, asking to be introduced to her.

They were being, she thought, over-familiar with Lady Laker.

She realised they were all betting on who would be the winner.

She could not help hoping that Lord Flore would not hear of what was taking place.

If he was annoyed with her for being in the Betting-Book at Whites, this would be far worse.

"You are the odds-on favourite, Old Girl!" she heard an over-dressed Beau say to Lady Laker. "If I lose my shirt on you, I shall ring your neck!"

"Don't you worry," Lady Laker answered. "I have never yet lost a race, a bet, or a man!"

There was a roar of laughter.

Malvina was not surprised when Sir Mortimer drew her away towards her own Phaeton.

She and Lady Laker were driving the race without a groom behind them.

They were to follow in the carriages which were coming along behind.

There would be, Malvina thought, quite a procession.

Some of the gentlemen from the St. James's Clubs were travelling in the very high Phaetons.

They made the one she was driving look like a pygmy.

There was no sign of Sir Hector.

A Referee who was an older and experienced man told Lady Laker and Malvina the rules of the race.

"No interference with your opponent," he said, "and keep on the direct road which leads almost straight from here to Potters Bar."

"Suppose we lose our way?" Malvina asked.

"There is no chance of that, Miss Maulton," he said in a kindly tone. "Guides have already gone ahead to keep you from turning off by mistake."

He smiled at her before he went on:

"When you reach Potters Bar, you will find the house on the other side of the village and the gates will be decorated so you cannot possibly miss them."

"Thank you," Malvina said.

"Are you both ready?" he asked. "Be careful when you first drive off not to become entangled with each other's vehicles."

He had a large white handkerchief in his hand.

He raised it high above his head so that they could both see it.

"One . . . two . . . three . . . go!" he shouted.

Both Phaetons started moving.

Malvina was very careful to drive slowly as they moved towards the exit from the Park.

She was aware by glancing at Lady Laker that she did in fact drive very well, but in a somewhat exaggerated fashion of which her father would not have approved.

Malvina sat upright, as he had taught her, holding the reins at exactly the right position.

She did not wave to those who cheered them as they went off.

Lady Laker was shouting at the gentlemen supporting her, making jokes about the race.

Sir Mortimer merely said quietly to Malvina:

"Good luck, and mind you, win! There is no question of your doing anything else."

Malvina hoped he was right.

Then she was moving swiftly through the traffic, towards the North.

The road was wide, so that a little later she was able to pass Lady Laker.

She heard her scream as she did so, but she was not certain what she said.

Then she settled down to drive swiftly, but at the same time carefully.

It was a lovely day, not too hot.

There was just enough wind to make anyone feel fresh and not too much sun to blind the eyes.

As she drove on, Malvina knew that Sir Mortimer had been right.

It would have been hard to find two more outstanding horses.

The two she had bought were also well-trained.

They moved together as if it were natural for them to do so.

Now they were away from the houses and out into the open country.

Malvina went a little faster.

She was still just ahead of Lady Laker.

She was aware that Her Ladyship was using her whip to force her horses to go faster than they wished.

A little farther on she passed Malvina, who made no attempt to stop her from doing so.

As she did so, Lady Laker turned her head and put out her tongue.

It was such a vulgar gesture that Malvina was astonished.

She was only glad that the large crowd of followers in their Phaetons, Chaises, and open carriages would not be aware of Lady Laker's behaviour.

'She is obviously very common!' she thought to herself.

Once again she felt apprehensively that she should not be taking part in this race.

Not with a woman like that.

If Lord Flore heard about it, he would certainly have a great deal to say.

'It is not his business!' she thought again with a toss of her head.

Yet she could not help feeling that in this instance he would be justified in scolding her.

She wished the race were over and she could return home.

Three-quarters-of-an-hour later they were nearing Potters Bar.

As they passed through the village where Malvina knew the Horse Fairs took place every year, the road widened.

It was then she pushed her horses forward and more or less gave them their heads.

They swept past Lady Laker with only a few inches to spare between the two vehicles.

Then, as she heard Lady Laker scream with fury, Malvina accelerated the pace.

The horses seemed to know almost without her encouragement exactly what was expected of them.

By the time the decorated gate and the crowd of people waiting to cheer were in sight, she knew she was well ahead and undoubtedly the winner.

She swept through the gate.

The men threw up their caps and the children waved handkerchiefs and flags.

Then she was driving between two lines of oak trees to where at the end she could see a rather ugly house.

In front of it was a tall white post.

She had to pass it to reach the court-yard, and she could see a number of men waiting there.

They took off their hats as she drove past them.

She drew her horses, which were only sweating slightly, to a stand-still.

A large, burly-looking man shook her warmly by the hand.

"Well done!" he exclaimed. "You have won the race, and I am very proud to meet you!"

Malvina thought this must be Sir Hector.

She put down the reins as she saw a groom go to the horses' heads and said:

"It was very exciting, and I feel I must thank you for letting me compete in your race."

"It is not mine, it is Sir Mortimer's," he said. "It was he who thought of it, and I bet he is 'cock-a-hoop' at finding he was right in choosing you!"

Malvina thought this was a different story from what Sir Mortimer had told her.

However, there was no time to think.

She was surrounded by men wanting to shake her hand.

She could also hear, now that she, too, had arrived, Lady Laker screeching with anger.

She declared the horses she had been given to drive were not good enough.

Malvina suddenly realised she was a little tired.

She was very dusty as the road had been dry.

When Lady Laker had been ahead, the dust from the wheels of her Phaeton had enveloped her like a cloud.

She got out of the Phaeton and walked up the steps of the house.

There appeared to be no hostess, and she said

to a servant at the top of the steps:

"I would like to wash, if you will show me to a bed-room."

He went ahead of her up the steps.

She could see that the house was badly furnished and in poor taste.

The pictures were not worth looking at and the curtains were of a somewhat vulgar colour.

The bed-room into which she was shown was luxurious, but curtained in the same crude manner.

The carpet was too bright.

There was, however, water with which to wash her face and hands.

A maid came to shake the dust from her bonnet.

Malvina had worn a plain, neat dust-coat which was very unlike Lady Laker's.

The only trimming on her bonnet was the ribbons.

"Will ye be puttin' on your bonnet again for luncheon, Ma'am?" the maid asked.

"I shall be much more comfortable without it," Malvina said. "What will the other ladies be doing?"

"There b'aint be any other ladies, Miss, jest gen'men."

Malvina looked surprised, but she did not say anything.

When she went downstairs it was to find at least twenty gentlemen in the Sitting-Room.

As the maid had said, there were no other ladies except herself and Lady Laker.

"Well, you won, and I suppose I should con-gratulate you," Lady Laker said sourly as Malvina came into the room.

"That is sporting, at any rate!" Sir Hector ex-claimed.

Putting a glass into Malvina's hand, he said:

"Have a drink, m'dear! And we all think you've done a splendid job!"

Malvina realised there was champagne in the glass, and she took a few sips because she was thirsty.

Everybody else seemed to be drinking as if they were parched.

She could only imagine it was because they had suffered so acutely from the dust.

When they were told that luncheon was ready, they moved into another large, ugly room.

Malvina noted that some of the gentlemen had already had too much to drink.

"I should not be here!" she told herself.

Once again she was hoping that Lord Flore would never hear of it.

chapter six

Malvina felt as if heavy black clouds were pressing on her and she could not move them away.

Gradually, there seemed to be a light flickering in the darkness.

She was aware that her lips felt very dry and her head was aching.

She tried to think where she could be, and remembered someone lifting a glass to her lips.

Then, as the darkness moved a little farther away, she recalled a man's voice, which she thought was Sir Mortimer's, saying:

"You must return the toast. Drink this up!"

He had pressed a glass into her hand.

She sipped it, knowing she did not like red wine.

Then she was aware that his hand had closed over hers, and incredibly he was forcing the wine down her throat.

Did he really do that?

She asked herself the question, and with an effort opened her eyes.

For a moment she could see nothing. There was a canopy over her head.

A feeble light came, she realised, from a fireplace.

She parted her lips, was aware her throat was very dry, and knew she had been drugged.

For a moment the idea was so horrifying that she shut her eyes.

She felt she had stepped into a nightmare from which it was difficult to wake up.

Her thoughts became clearer, and she forced her eyes open again.

Now she was aware that behind a heavy curtain beside the bed there was a lighted candle.

She could see that she was in the same bedroom in which she had washed when she arrived after the race.

What had happened? Why was she here?

It was then that a streak of fear ran through her.

With what was a superhuman effort, she sat up.

She had been lying on the bed in the gown she had worn at luncheon, and only her shoes had been removed.

She looked across the room.

Now she could see there was a table which was covered with a cloth by the fireplace, and on it were arranged some covered dishes.

There was also a plate, a knife, a fork, and what looked like a coffee-pot with a cup and a saucer beside it.

She thought if she could drink something she would be able to think more clearly.

Very slowly, because it was difficult to move, she got off the bed.

After holding on to the end of it to support herself, she walked towards the table.

She reached it, and now the light seemed a little brighter.

She could see it was a coffee-pot.

She put out her hand towards it.

She realised her fingers were trembling and she had to hold on to the pot with both hands to pour the coffee into the cup.

It was thick and black, but not too hot, and she drank thirstily.

It was then the darkness in her head receded.

Now she was strong enough to know that something terrible had happened.

She had been drugged and brought upstairs to the bed-room she had used before — but why?

She tried to remember if Sir Hector had given her the cheque he had promised.

She thought perhaps she had been kidnapped for the money.

Then, as she poured herself out another cup of coffee, she had a far more sinister idea.

She tried to open the door, and found it was locked.

It was then with an overwhelming sense of shock she knew who had taken her prisoner, and why.

She drank the coffee and sat down, not in the comfortable chair by the fireside, but on the stool in front of the dressing-table.

The curtains had been pulled and she knew it would be dark outside.

She must have been in a drugged sleep for many hours.

"What am I to do?" she asked herself.

It was then in a sudden panic she knew that she wanted Lord Flore.

Only he could save her from Sir Mortimer.

She knew now, without anyone telling her so, that it was he who had plotted this from the very beginning.

It had not been Sir Hector's race.

Sir Mortimer had arranged it so that he could get her away from her grandmother, also from Lord Flore, of whom he was jealous.

He would keep her here until she promised to marry him.

She could see the whole plot as if it were laid out in front of her, like the plan Lord Flore had drawn for the race-course.

She got to her feet and walked to the window, pulling back the curtains.

She looked out, wondering if this was a means of escape.

But the windows, and there were two of them, looked out over a garden at the back of the house.

There was a straight fall of perhaps forty feet to the ground.

The window was open, and she could see the stars overhead, and everything was very still.

She thought that the Drawing-Room in which

they had met before luncheon looked out in the same direction.

It was so quiet that she guessed the other people had driven back to London.

They had left her here alone.

Then she gave a little gasp.

She knew there would be one person left at any rate, one person who had manipulated her as if she were a puppet in his hands, and one person who had everything to gain by keeping her a prisoner.

"Help me . . . Papa," she prayed. "What . . . am I to . . . do?"

Then she remembered that her father was dead and could not help her.

There was one person who was alive, one person who could stand up to Sir Mortimer, one person who would disapprove violently of what was happening to her.

Because she was so frightened, her whole being cried out to him.

She imagined him in the Priory.

He would be poring over his plan for the racecourse, having no idea of the peril she was in.

"Save . . . me! Save . . . me!" she cried in her heart, and knew at that moment that she loved him.

Of course she loved him!

How could she do anything else when he was so much a man.

He was so different from the weak idiots she

had despised because they wanted to marry her only for her money.

She thought of Sir Mortimer, and shuddered.

How could she have been so foolish?

She had let him persuade her into driving in a race which had resulted in her being talked about in the way Lord Flore most disliked.

Now she could remember the noisy manner in which the smartly-dressed gentlemen had acclaimed Lady Laker.

They had wagered large sums of money that she would win the race.

They had also kissed her, in what Malvina had thought was a very vulgar manner before the race started.

It had been worse at luncheon.

She could remember now man after man raising his glass to her and to Lady Laker.

Then he would toss the whole contents down his throat before he threw the glass over his shoulder.

It had smashed in smithereens behind him.

She had thought then how angry Lord Flore would be, and how severely he would lecture her.

He would have been right, completely right, and she would not have listened to him!

"What . . . am I to . . . do?" she asked again desperately.

At that moment there was the sound of a key being turned in the lock.

The door opened.

It was, as she expected, Sir Mortimer.

He came into the room and she thought he looked sinister.

There was an expression on his face which made her shake inside herself.

"You are awake!" he exclaimed. "Well, my adorable little Heiress, you are my guest, and now the cards are down on the table!"

"I do not know what you mean," Malvina said bravely, "and how dare you drug me in that outrageous fashion and keep me here against my will!"

"There was no other way of making sure you married me," Sir Mortimer replied.

"You must be crazy if you think I would marry you!" Malvina retorted. "I suppose what you are really asking is that I give you half my fortune!"

Sir Mortimer laughed, and it was an unpleasant sound.

"Why should I take half a loaf when I possess the whole?"

Malvina stared at him.

There was an evil smile on his lips as he said:

"To-morrow, all my friends who have left here to return to London will know where you spent the night."

He saw the expression of horror on Malvina's face.

He gave a chuckle before he went on:

"It is no use, my pretty, I hold every trump-card, and a Special Licence. We will be married after breakfast, then return to receive the congratulations of our friends and relations."

"How can . . . you be so . . . appalling . . . so absolutely . . . revolting!" Malvina exclaimed.

"Very easily," Sir Mortimer replied, "when it is a question of being in possession of your fortune, and, of course, you!"

"You can have all my fortune and spare me the humiliation of being your wife!" Malvina snapped.

Sir Mortimer laughed again.

"That is what I might have expected you to say, but your fortune, my dear little innocent, consists not only of what is in the Bank now, but what is coming in year after year and, thanks to your father's brilliant brain, is also increasing."

"And do you really think," Malvina flared, "that I would allow you to touch money which my father worked so hard to obtain?"

"You have no choice," Sir Mortimer replied. "If you refuse to marry me, there is quite a simple answer to that. I will ravish you before marriage! Even your grandmother will then advise you to marry the father of your child!"

Malvina clenched her fingers together until her knuckles turned white.

She wanted to scream, and go on screaming.

But her brain told her no one would come to her rescue.

She would only humiliate herself more than she was already.

She looked at Sir Mortimer.

She wondered how she had ever been so stupid to think of him as an ordinary civilised being.

She knew from his expression that he was glorying in his own cleverness and feeling triumphant that she was helpless in his power.

She pressed her lips together to stop herself from screaming abuse at him.

It would take her down to his level.

Then in a deep and much more dangerous tone of voice he said:

"You are very desirable! Why should we wait for a lot of 'mumbo-jumbo' from a Parson? If nothing else, I will teach you to desire me, my pretty one!"

As he spoke he took a step towards her.

With a swiftness born of terror Malvina snatched up the knife from the table.

She backed away from him towards the window.

"If you are really thinking of trying to kill me," Sir Mortimer said mockingly, "let me assure you I would come off best in that fight!"

Malvina lifted the knife to her throat.

"If you touch me," she said, "I will kill myself! I will slash my jugular vein! I would rather be dead than allow you to set one finger on me!"

She spoke so vehemently that Sir Mortimer was still.

There was a long silence. Finally he said:

"I might have expected such dramatics!"

"I am not being dramatic," Malvina said, "I am merely saying that if you come one step nearer, you will have my dead body to explain away."

She was standing very straight with the point of the knife, which was sharp, actually touching her skin.

"They were right when they called you a 'Tigress'!" Sir Mortimer said with a nasty note in his voice. "But, by God, when you are married to me, I will tame you. To begin with, it will be a somewhat painful process!"

Malvina did not move and he said slowly:

"Very well, have it your own way. But you will marry me to-morrow morning, or return to London labelled a 'Scarlet Woman.' And how the gossips will enjoy tearing you to shreds!"

He did not wait for Malvina to reply.

He walked out of the bed-room, slamming the door behind him.

She heard the key turn in the lock.

There was the sound of his footsteps going down the passage.

Only when she could hear him no longer did she collapse to the floor.

The knife slipped from her hand and she covered her face.

She was trying desperately not to faint with the horror of what had occurred.

She fought against the darkness that seemed to be descending upon her again, and cried out to Lord Flore:

"Save me . . . save me! I love you . . . save . . . me!"

Lord Flore, accompanied by the Earl, arrived at the Maulton stables at seven o'clock.

He was surprised to see Rosette waiting for them.

"You have really got up in time!" the Earl exclaimed with delight. "You are wonderful!"

"You asked . . . me to come . . . with you," Rosette said rather shyly.

"I was longing for you to do so," the Earl replied fervently.

The grooms had the horses already saddled, and they rode away towards the flat land.

Lord Flore was soon aware that this morning was rather different from other mornings.

The Earl kept looking at Rosette instead of concentrating on his riding.

She blushed very prettily at almost everything he said to her.

About a quarter-of-a-mile later Lord Flore said he had business to do.

He rode away alone.

As he did so, he told himself with a smile that Malvina's match-making was bearing fruit.

But not where he was concerned.

He was, in fact, disappointed that she had not appeared this morning as he had expected.

There were various things he wanted to discuss.

It was unlike her, he thought, to lie in, unless she had gone to bed late the previous night.

He reached the part of the grounds where he intended the race-course to be.

He had made a careful survey to see what shrubs and trees would have to be removed.

There were one or two things about Malvina's land he wanted to talk over with her.

When finally he returned to the stables he said to Hodgson:

"Is Miss Maulton riding this morning?"

"Ah, no, M'Lord," Hodgson replied, " 'Er be gone orf to London."

"Gone to London?" Lord Flore exclaimed in surprise.

"Yes, M'Lord, 'er went off soon after Your Lor'ship went ridin' wi' that Sir Mortimer, drivin' two of our new 'orses. Oi only 'opes 'e knows 'ow to 'andle 'em."

"With Sir Mortimer Smythe?" Lord Flore questioned sharply.

"Tha's roight, M'Lord, an' 'e keep two o' t'horses in London as shoulda bin back 'ere."

"I do not understand what you are saying," Lord Flore said. "Why should Sir Mortimer Smythe prevent two horses from arriving as was expected?"

"Oi thinks as Dickson, 'oo was in charge, can tell ye that better'n me, M'Lord."

He called Dickson.

Lord Flore was aware he was the Second Groom and a very experienced man.

" 'Is Lordship wan' ye to tell 'im," Hodgson said, "wot be 'appening in London 'bout our new 'orses."

"Sir Mortimer says, M'Lord," Dickson explained, "that th' two 'orses who was th' best at being driven should take part in a race."

"A race?" Lord Flore ejaculated. "What race?"

"Well, Sir, th' grooms at Berkeley Square were a-sayin' it were to take place ter-day, an' Miss Malvina 'ad challenged Lady Laker for a huge sum o' money — thousands, it were!"

"I do not believe it!" Lord Flore said beneath his breath.

He questioned Dickson until he realised the man knew no more.

Then he told himself it was none of his business.

The servants would certainly talk if they thought he was making a fuss.

He therefore mounted his own horse and rode back to the Priory.

As he went he was wondering what mischief Malvina was up to now.

Why had she not confided in him?

When he arrived, he walked through the Great Hall and into the Abbot's Room in search of the Earl.

When he opened the door the young people were standing in the window, and sprang apart guiltily.

It was clear to Lord Flore that David had been kissing Rosette.

For a moment they both looked startled.

Then David said:

"Congratulate me, Shelton! I am the happiest man in the world!"

Lord Flore held out his hand.

"It is the best news I have ever heard!" he said. "And I know you will both be very happy."

"Oh, thank you, thank you!" Rosette said. "But I will not take David away from you, and perhaps we could both help to restore this beautiful house."

Lord Flore smiled.

"It is certainly an idea, and something which we will have to think about."

They smiled at each other, and he knew they were wanting him to leave them alone.

But there was something he had to know first.

"Tell me, David," he said, "have you heard of a Lady Laker?"

The Earl considered for a moment.

"The only Laker I know," he said after a moment, "is Lily Laker. She is one of the performers at Astley's Amphitheatre, and is an absolute wizard with the Circus horses!"

He knew Astley had started a Circus near Westminster Bridge in 1772.

It was followed by his Amphitheatre, which was famous throughout the world.

But a woman performer was certainly not the right company for Malvina.

"That is all I wanted to know," he said aloud. "Enjoy yourselves!"

He realised that even before he had left the room, Rosette had moved back into David's arms.

He hurried upstairs and changed from his riding-clothes into those he wore in London.

Then he rode back to the stables at Maulton Park.

"I want two of your best horses," he said to Hodgson, "and the fastest vehicle you have."

Hodgson scratched his head.

"Miss Maulton's took it," he said, "but we've a D'Orcy Carricle which is new."

He pronounced it wrongly, but Lord Flore knew it had been designed by the dashing Count D'Orsay and it was very light.

"That will do," he said.

"Ye be goin' to London, M'Lord?"

"I am going to find Miss Maulton, Hodgson, I think she may be in trouble, but do not say anything about it to anyone in the house."

" 'Course not, M'Lord," Hodgson agreed, " 'an' 'Er Ladyship's jus' ordered 'er carriage for a'ter luncheon, so Oi 'spects Miss Maulton be meetin' 'er at Berkeley Square."

"I sincerely hope so," Lord Flore replied.

Lord Flore reached London just after two o'clock.

The Head Groom in the stables at Berkeley Square confirmed what Dickson had said.

He knew the race had started in the Regents Park and at what time the competitors had left.

What he did not know exactly was where they were going.

Lord Flore left the Curricle and took a Hackney Carriage to Whites Club.

He deliberately did not ask any questions about the race.

He had luncheon with two of his friends, and waited.

As the hours passed, he read the newspapers.

Also he talked to several friends with whom he had been at School.

But anyone who knew him very well would have realised that he was in fact very tense.

It was nearly six o'clock when a number of the over-dressed and noisy young Bucks came into the Club.

They threw themselves in what appeared to be an exhausted manner down into the comfortable leather armchairs in the Morning-Room.

A young man Lord Flore did not know asked: "Well? Who won?"

"The heiress!" was the reply. "And was Lily angry! But there was nothing she could do about it. The 'Tigress' had better horses, and there is no doubt she drives dam' well!"

Lord Flore rose and walked across the room.

"Forgive me for being curious," he said, "but I heard about this race and I am sorry not to have watched it."

"You missed a treat!" the man who had been talking replied. "I never drank a better claret than we had at luncheon."

"Where was that?" Lord Flore enquired.

"At Bill Tiverton's house the other side of Potters Bar," was the reply. "You know — it is where he keeps all his pretty 'Bits o' Muslin.' There has been at least half-a-dozen of them through there. Mimi has lasted longer than

153

most, and he has taken her to Paris."

Someone in the party, which had now in-creased, made a witty remark.

There was a burst of laughter.

"What has become of the drivers of this un-usual race?" Lord Flore asked conversationally.

"Lily Laker has gone off with Sir Hector, as you might have expected," was the reply, "and the heiress passed out!"

"Passed out?" Lord Flore asked sharply.

"It might have been exhaustion, or the wine, or both!" the young man replied. "Anyway, Smythe carried her away and I expect he will bring her back later."

There was a rather lewd remark from one of the other Beaux as to how much later was later.

Lord Flore tightened his lips.

Unobtrusively he moved away and out of the Club.

He had found out what he wanted to know.

It was imperative that he should find Malvina immediately.

When he reached Berkeley Square he learnt without going into the house that the Dowager Countess had arrived.

In the stables Lord Flore asked for two fresh horses to draw the Curricle, and for a groom to come with him.

He was just about to depart when Malvina's Phaeton, driven by her groom, came into the yard.

Before anyone else could move, Lord Flore

was beside the groom in the driving-seat.

"Has Miss Maulton come back with you?" he asked.

"Nay, Sir," the groom replied. "The gen'man as took 'er to Tiverton 'Ouse says as I weren't wanted, an' ter take t'horses home."

Lord Flore made no reply.

He sprang up into the Curricle and picked up the reins.

The groom who was to go with him climbed up behind and he set off.

As he did so there was an expression on his face which would have warned those who had worked with him in the East that he was in a furious temper.

As it was still early in the year, it was almost dark by the time he reached Potters Bar.

He had a little trouble in finding the way to Tiverton House.

The groom sitting behind him had suggested they should stop and ask, but Lord Flore had refused.

He now drove his horses slower, and slower still until they passed through the now-deserted gates.

These were still decorated with flags and bunting.

Before they reached the end of the drive he pulled in his horses.

He looked ahead at the house.

He thought, as Malvina had, that it was an ugly building.

He knew exactly what its owner was like if he kept it for rowdy parties and a procession of "Cyprians."

The idea of Malvina entering such a place made him even more angry than he was already.

Quite a number of lights could be seen on the Ground Floor, but only a few in the upper floors.

Lord Flore handed the groom the reins.

"I am going to explore," he said. "Watch the front-door. When I want you I will wave a white handkerchief."

He looked up at the sky.

The stars were coming out one by one.

The last vestiges of light had disappeared behind the oak trees.

Lord Flore got out of the Curricle.

He put his top-hat down on the seat, then walked in the direction of the house.

He kept carefully in the shade of the bushes and off the drive itself.

Looking in through the windows he discovered that what servants there were had retired to the kitchen quarters.

In the Dining-Room he saw the lights were being put out.

Those behind the curtains of what he suspected was a Sitting-Room were still shining.

He found as he expected that the front-door had been shut and locked for the night.

He let himself into the house by deftly breaking a pane of glass in one of the downstairs windows.

Then he walked along a corridor to the room in which he felt sure he would find Sir Mortimer Smythe.

He was not mistaken.

As he opened the door Sir Mortimer was sitting comfortably in an armchair in front of the fire with a glass of brandy beside him.

There was a look of satisfaction on his face.

As Lord Flore entered, he did not for a moment look up, thinking it was a servant.

Then, as Lord Flore stood looking at him, he raised his eyes.

For a moment he seemed frozen into immobility before he asked furiously:

"What the Devil are you doing here?"

"That is what I have come to ask you!" Lord Flore said in an ominous tone. "What have you done with her?"

Sir Mortimer put down his glass of brandy and rose to his feet.

"Now, look here, Flore —" he began.

"Answer me!" Lord Flore interrupted.

He reached Sir Mortimer, and as he did so he hit him, knocking him down on one knee.

"How dare you strike me!" Sir Mortimer shouted. "If you want a fight, we will fight like gentlemen, with pistols!"

"You are no gentleman, and I will fight you now!" Lord Flore replied. "Tell me where you have put Malvina!"

"She is going to be my wife, and you have no right to interfere!" Sir Mortimer yelled.

It was then that Lord Flore hit him on the point of the chin.

The blow lifted him off the ground so that he fell backwards, crashed, and did not move.

Lord Flore made certain he was unconscious, then walked out of the room.

Shutting the door behind him, he went up the stairs.

He tried two doors which opened easily before he found one which was locked, but the key was in the door.

As he turned it, Malvina heard the sound and rose to her feet.

She groped for the knife as she did so.

When Lord Flore opened the door she was standing stiffly, as she had before, with the knife at her throat.

For a moment she just stared at him.

Then as if she suddenly realised he was really there, she gave a cry that echoed round the room.

Dropping the knife, she ran towards him.

"You have . . . come! You . . . have . . . come!" she cried. "I prayed you . . . would save . . . me!"

She flung herself against him, and his arms went round her.

He held her very close.

She looked up at him, the tears running down her cheeks.

"Y-you . . . have . . . c-come!" she repeated.

"And . . . I have been so . . . terribly . . . terribly frightened!"

"How could you have done anything so absolutely stupid?" Lord Flore asked angrily.

Then, as if he could not help himself, his lips took possession of hers.

chapter seven

For a moment Malvina could not believe what was happening.

Then as Lord Flore's lips held her captive, she felt as if her whole body melted into his.

She became a part of him.

His kisses made her feel that there was a warm wave moving through her body.

It gave her sensations she had never known before.

It was a rapture and an ecstasy that exceeded anything she had dreamt of as love.

It was so wonderful that nothing else in the world mattered except him and his lips.

Finally, after what seemed a very long time, Lord Flore raised his head.

He looked down at her.

Her cheeks were still wet with tears, but the radiance in her eyes was dazzling.

He thought no one could look more beautiful and at the same time pathetic.

"I love you . . . I love . . . you!" Malvina whispered. "And I . . . thought I . . . would have to . . . k-kill myself!"

Lord Flore's arms tightened.

Then he asked:

"That swine has not hurt you?"

"N-no . . . but I prayed for . . . you to . . . save me."

His lips touched her forehead.

"Let us get out of this mess!" he said. "Where is your coat?"

Malvina felt too bewildered to answer him.

Releasing her, he walked to the wardrobe and pulled it open.

Her coat was hanging there, and he took it down and picked up her bonnet.

He put his arm around her.

When they went through the door he realised she was trembling.

He knew, although she did not say so, that she was afraid of encountering Sir Mortimer.

"He will not trouble you," he said.

Malvina looked up at him.

"Y-you . . . you have not . . . killed him?"

"It is what he deserves!" Lord Flore replied. "But he is alive."

He took her to the front-door and unbolted it.

Going outside, he pulled a handkerchief from his pocket and waved it.

By this time the stars were bright with a moon creeping up the sky.

He knew it was easy for the groom to see him.

A few seconds later the horses came into the courtyard.

"Stay here!" Lord Flore ordered Malvina.

He went down the steps and helped the groom raise the hood which covered the two seats in front of the Curricle.

Then he helped Malvina down the steps.

As he picked up the reins, the groom jumped up behind and they drove off.

Once Malvina knew they could not be seen or heard, she moved closer to Lord Flore.

She put her head against his shoulder.

She was aware of little but the wonder of his kisses.

They made her feel as if she were disembodied and floating in the sky among the stars.

Only as they turned out through the gate did she say in a small, hesitating voice:

"H-how did you . . . find me? I was so . . . afraid that . . . you would . . . never even . . . guess where . . . I was."

"It is a long story," Lord Flore said, "and I have to get you back to London."

Malvina made a little murmur which was one of happiness, and he went on:

"You have to be well enough to ride in Rotten Row to-morrow morning, soon after eight o'clock, so you had better try to sleep."

"R-ride in . . . Rotten Row?" Malvina asked incredulously. "But . . . why? What for?"

"To make sure that your friends, and of course your enemies, realise you spent the night in London," Lord Flore explained. "You were in your own house and chaperoned by your grandmother."

Malvina drew in her breath.

She understood exactly what he was saying.

Of course the other guests at the luncheon-party would have been aware that while they had returned to London, she was left behind.

Furthermore, she would not trust Sir Mortimer not to have confided in his closest friends what he intended to do.

Only Lord Flore, she thought, could have thought of a way to confound the gossips.

They would be only too ready to condemn her for what they thought had happened.

There was a long silence.

Then she said in a very small voice:

"Are you . . . very angry . . . with me?"

"*Very* angry!" Lord Flore replied. "But we will also talk about that to-morrow!"

"I . . . I want to tell you . . . what happened . . . and why I . . . behaved so . . . foolishly."

"I will listen to-morrow," he said, "but now I have to concentrate on saving you not only from that Devil, who I will see is turned out of every decent Club to which he belongs, but also to make sure that whatever lies he tells are not believed by anyone who matters."

Malvina pressed her cheek against him.

"You are . . . wonderful!" she said. "And I know it was very . . . very foolish of me not to have . . . listened to you when . . . you told me not . . . to get myself . . . talked about."

Lord Flore did not reply.

But she thought it must be an effort on his

part not to lecture her.

At the same time, he had kissed her.

She knew now that she loved him so over-whelmingly that all she wanted to do was to please him.

He was driving the horses very fast.

She knew he did not want to talk, so she shut her eyes.

She thought of the sensations he had aroused in her, which she could still feel in her breast and on her lips.

"I . . . love you . . . I . . . love you!" she said in her heart.

To-morrow he would kiss her again.

Only when they had reached London and were only a short distance from Berkeley Square did Malvina ask:

"Did David come to London with you?"

"No," Lord Flore replied. "I left him at the Priory, too happy to think of anything but him-self!"

"Too happy?"

"He and the little heiress you produced for me are to be married!"

"Oh, I am glad!" Malvina cried. "I thought when they were dancing together that they looked very happy, and now all David's prob-lems will be over!"

Lord Flore did not answer.

She wondered if he was thinking that his were still unsolved.

She knew then there was a very easy way to do that, but she dared not suggest it.

She was silent for a long time before she asked:

"Will you ride with me to-morrow morning?"

"Certainly not!" Lord Flore replied. "You will ride with a groom, and if you see anybody who was in that vulgar house, or who saw you taking part in the race, you will greet them politely and mention casually that you were very tired after it was all over, and it made you late getting back to London."

He had obviously thought out exactly what she had to do.

Malvina said softly:

"I will do as . . . you tell me . . . but when shall . . . I see you . . . again?"

"I believe you have been invited to a luncheon party," Lord Flore said, "which you will attend. I will call on you at three o'clock."

Malvina wanted to protest that she wanted to see him before that.

But by now they were in Berkeley Square.

Lord Flore drew up outside her house.

The groom jumped down to knock on the door which was opened by a sleepy night-footman.

Lord Flore helped Malvina out of the Curricle.

She clung to his hand, looking up at him pleadingly.

"Good-night, Malvina!" he said firmly. "I am taking the Curricle round to the Mews and will order your horse for eight o'clock."

She tried to hold on to him, but he turned away.

As the footman shut the door she walked very slowly up the stars.

She thought if there was a light under her grandmother's door she would have to go in and explain why she was so late.

To her relief, however, there was only darkness.

She went to her own bed-room.

She did not ring for her maid, but undressed and got into bed.

She wanted to stay awake, thinking of Lord Flore and of how he had saved her.

She fell asleep from sheer exhaustion but dreamt of his kisses.

Malvina was awoken at a quarter after seven.

Although she wanted to protest that she was too tired to go riding, she knew she must obey Lord Flore's orders.

She felt better by the time she reached Rotten Row.

She forced herself to smile at everybody she knew.

Quite a number of men whose names she did not know, but who had been present at the luncheon, came up to say:

"You drove brilliantly yesterday, but you must have been tired. What time did you get back to London?"

She knew it was an important question, and

she answered lightly:

"I arrived soon after you did, and I admit to sleeping the whole way back!"

They laughed at that.

Then two of the more ardent Bucks rode a little way with her.

They paid her compliments.

They also asked her to promise them a dance at the Ball she was attending this evening.

It was after nine o'clock when she returned home.

She felt as if her smile were fixed on her face.

At the same time, she knew the suspicions that had been in some of the men's eyes when they first saw her had vanished.

"Shelton will be very proud of me," she told herself, and thought his name sounded like music.

"I love him! I love him!" her horse's hoofs were saying as she rode home.

"I love him!" she told herself as she changed into a smart gown for the luncheon.

"He saved me!" she wanted to tell her grandmother.

The Dowager Countess lectured her for travelling to London alone with Sir Mortimer and for being out so late.

Malvina longed to say how marvellous Lord Flore had been in finding her.

If he had not done so, she would at this moment be lying dead.

But she knew he would be angry if she told

anyone what had occurred.

She therefore apologised very prettily to her grandmother, who finally forgave her.

When they arrived back at Berkeley Square the Dowager said she was going to rest.

"We have another Ball to-night," she sighed. "I am getting too old for these late nights!"

Malvina took off her smart bonnet and tidied her hair.

She looked in the mirror.

She thought the gown she was wearing was one of the very prettiest she owned.

She had put it on especially for Lord Flore because she wanted him to think she looked pretty.

She was still scrutinising her appearance when a footman knocked on her bed-room door to say:

"Lord Flore has called t' see you, Miss Malvina!"

Malvina did not answer.

She only ran to the door and, passing the servant, hurried down the stairs.

She knew Lord Flore would have been shown into the Sitting-Room on the Ground Floor.

It looked out onto the garden.

She had taken the trouble before they went out to luncheon to see that there were plenty of flowers there.

She went into the room and the door closed behind her.

He was standing by the window, and she felt her heart turn several somersaults because he looked so handsome.

"Good-afternoon, Malvina!" he said. "I hope you are rested?"

She wanted to run across the room and throw herself into his arms.

But he had spoken in an ordinary voice that seemed somehow cold and distant.

She walked slowly towards him, hoping he would hold out his arms.

Then as she reached him she said a little hesitatingly:

"H-how . . . can I begin to . . . thank you —"

"It would be a mistake to even think of what occurred yesterday!" he interrupted. "It is something, Malvina, that you have to forget and only make sure that it never happens again."

"But . . . I want to . . . tell you —" she began again.

"No!" he said. "I have told you to forget it. It was a disaster from beginning to end but, fortunately, unless you talk about it, there will be little harm done!"

"But . . . suppose . . . Sir Mortimer . . . ?" Malvina murmured.

"I will deal with him," Lord Flore said grimly, "and all you have to do is to forget he even exists!"

"I will . . . try," Malvina said, "but . . . I have something to . . . say to you."

"What is it?" Lord Flore asked.

She moved a little nearer to him.

Then she said:

"I love . . . you! When you saved me . . . and

when you . . . kissed me . . . I knew then that I . . . loved you!"

She thought Lord Flore would put his arms around her, but instead he turned away.

"That is also something you have to forget!" he said harshly.

"But . . . why? I do not . . . understand."

"For one minute I think we both lost our heads. You were frightened, and I was afraid of what I might find. Now we must get back to where we were before: partners in building a race-course — but nothing more!"

Malvina felt as if her heart had stopped beating.

Could Lord Flore have kissed her and then say he had no further interest in her?

And yet, instinctively, she knew he was not saying what he felt.

He could not have kissed her as he had and she could not have felt that she was a part of him unless he loved her too.

She looked at his profile silhouetted against the green of a tree outside.

He could hardly hear her say in a whisper:

"Please, Shelton . . . will you . . . marry me?"

Lord Flore stiffened. Then he said angrily:

"That is something you should not ask a man, but a man should ask you."

"But . . . you have not . . . asked me . . . and . . . and I love you!"

"The answer is 'No'!"

"But . . . why? Surely you love me . . . just a little . . . and I swear if you marry me . . . I will be the sort of . . . wife you want . . . quiet, gentle, and . . . obedient!"

Lord Flore did not answer.

She knew he was standing as stiff and still as if he had been turned to stone.

"Please, Shelton . . . please . . . !"

There was no response.

With a little sob she said:

"If you will not . . . marry me . . . may I . . . live with you . . . as your . . . mistress?"

Lord Flore turned round.

She thought she had never seen a man look so angry.

"How dare you!" he raged. "How dare you suggest anything so wrong, so wicked, so degrading! As your father's daughter, you ought to be ashamed of yourself!"

He reached out his hands as he spoke and put them on her shoulders.

"How can I make you behave?" he asked furiously.

"I . . . I do not want to . . . behave!" Malvina replied. "And I know you are refusing to marry me . . . only because of my . . . tiresome money! I hate it . . . do you hear? I hate it!"

She sobbed and went on:

"If it stops you from loving me . . . then I will . . . give it away to . . . every man who . . . asks me for it! I will pay their debts . . . and I will make the beggars in the streets into millionaires . . . and for all I care . . . Sir Mortimer . . . c-can have the r-rest!"

It was then Lord Flore shook her so that her head rocked backwards and forwards.

The pins dropped out of her hair so that it fell like a golden cloud over her shoulders.

"You are not to talk like that!" he stormed. "You will spend your money properly and behave like the Lady you are supposed to be!"

"I will . . . not! I . . . will . . . not!" Malvina sobbed defiantly.

Now she was crying, and she was helpless in Lord Flore's hands.

Suddenly, as if he realised how rough he was being, he stopped shaking her, but his hands were still on her shoulders.

Then, as he looked at her tear-filled eyes and pale cheeks, something seemed to break within him.

"Oh, my God!" he exclaimed, and pulled her roughly against him.

Then he was kissing her, kissing her violently, fiercely, demandingly.

His lips hurt her, but Malvina was not afraid.

This was what she had wanted; this was what he was taking away from her.

She knew if he really did not love her, she had no wish to go on living.

Then his lips became more possessive, more passionate.

A streak of ecstasy seeped through her body like lightning.

The darkness was over and a light that could have come only from the stars seemed to blind her.

He drew her closer still, and her heart was singing.

She knew he had carried her into a special Heaven, where there was only his love and him.

After a long time he raised his head to look down at her.

Then he was kissing her again, kissing her until she felt she must die not from fear, but from sheer happiness.

Only when they were both breathless did Lord Flore say, and his voice sounded very deep and unsteady:

"How can you make me feel like this?"

"Like . . . what?" she questioned.

"I love you."

Malvina gave a little cry of happiness and hid her face against him.

"I suppose," he said, "I shall have to look after you."

"That . . . is what I . . . want you to . . . do," she whispered.

"God knows what I am letting myself in for!" he remarked.

Before she could answer, his lips found hers again.

Then, as they heard the door open and moved apart, the Butler announced:

"A gentleman from India to see you, Miss Malvina!"

Aware that her hair was tumbling over her shoulders and there were tears on her face, Malvina turned towards the window.

Instinctively Lord Flore moved in front of her.

He faced the man who was ushered into the room.

He was an Indian, wearing his native dress under a rather ugly Western tweed coat.

He was carrying a case in his hand, and as Lord Flore moved across the room towards him he said:

"I come to ask *Sahib* Maulton's daughter the address of *Sahib* Shelton Flore."

He stopped speaking suddenly and looked at Lord Flore.

"But you *are* Shelton Flore, *Sahib!*" he exclaimed.

"I am!" Lord Flore confirmed. "And surely, I have seen you before?"

"I am Asaf, *Sahib,* Personal Attendant to His Highness the Maharajah of Kapinwar."

"But of course!" Lord Flore exclaimed, holding out his hand. "I remember you well. How is His Highness?"

Asaf's smile vanished.

"His Highness dead, *Sahib!*"

"Dead?" Lord Flore replied. "I am very sorry to hear that! He was a great man!"

"Very great, *Sahib,* thanks to you and *Sahib* Maulton."

While they were talking, Malvina had pinned her hair in place and wiped her face.

Now she came from the window.

As she reached Lord Flore he said:

"This gentleman has come here in search of

me. He is Asaf, whom I knew in India."

Malvina held out her hand.

"I heard you speak of my father," she said.

"Magnamus Maulton very kind man," the Indian replied. "He send Shelton Flore *Sahib* to help His Highness. He help us all and His Highness very grateful."

Malvina smiled and looked at Lord Flore.

"How did you help the Maharajah?" she asked.

"I found him a Diamond Mine!" Lord Flore replied.

Malvina looked at him incredulously, and the Indian said:

"Yes, yes, that true, and His Highness wish thank you. When he die, he leave this for you, *Sahib,* and I bring it to you all the way from India."

"That was very kind of you, Asaf," Lord Flore said, "and of course I shall treasure anything His Highness left for me."

The Indian looked around him.

Seeing a small table beside one of the arm chairs, he put the case he held in his hand on it.

"I guard this with my life, *Sahib,*" he said to Lord Flore.

"Then of course I must thank you," Lord Flore replied.

The Indian was drawing a key from somewhere around his waist.

As he unlocked the case Malvina was sure it contained a statue of a god, perhaps a beautifully fashioned one of Krishna dancing.

She had seen so many of them when she was in India.

Her father possessed quite a collection, some of them ornamented with precious stones.

The Indian put his hand on the top of the case. "This, *Sahib*," he said to Lord Flore, "come with His Highness's most grateful thanks from the depths of his heart for what you do for him."

Lord Flore bowed his head in acknowledgement.

Then, with a theatrical gesture, the Indian opened the case.

Malvina was disappointed.

The contents were not what she had expected, but appeared to be merely a collection of pebbles.

Then Lord Flore exclaimed:

"Diamonds!"

"From the Mine, *Sahib!*" the Indian said triumphantly. "Some very large — all very, very valuable!"

"And — they are — for me?" Lord Flore asked as if he could hardly believe it.

"His Highness's last wish, *Sahib*, and in His Highness's Will he say ten percent of all we dig, year after year, come to you!"

Asaf gave a little laugh.

"*Sahib* Maulton called Mr. Ten Percent; now you same name."

Lord Flore drew in his breath.

"I find it hard to know what to say."

Malvina put out her hand to touch one of the "pebbles."

"Are they really diamonds?" she asked

"Very fine, very clear! Finest diamonds in India!" Asaf replied.

There was silence until Lord Flore said:

"You have come a long way, and I think now you should have something to eat before we have a further talk about His Highness's death, and his kind thoughts of me."

"That be very nice, *Sahib*."

"Then come with me, Asaf," Lord Flore said. "I know that Miss Maulton's Secretary will look after you, and when you are rested, we will have our talk."

He opened the door and the Indian followed him out into the corridor.

When she was alone, Malvina stared at the diamonds, touching first one, then another.

She knew when they were cut they would be of very great value.

She understood exactly what it would mean to Lord Flore to receive ten percent of everything the Mine produced, year after year.

She heard the door open, and held her breath.

Lord Flore came into the room and shut the door behind him.

Just for a moment he stood looking at her.

She had no idea that the sunshine coming through the window haloed her golden hair, turning its curls into tiny flames of fire.

There was an anxious look in her eyes.

Then, as he smiled, she knew that everything was all right.

She did not move, but he walked slowly towards her, and when he reached her he said very quietly:

"Now I can ask you properly — will you marry me, my darling?"

Malvina made a little sound that was half a laugh and half a sob as she said:

"N-now that you are . . . so rich . . . you can marry . . . anybody in the . . . world . . . and the Priory can . . . look like a Palace."

"You have not answered me," Lord Flore said.

"I . . . I love you," Malvina replied, "and . . . if I cannot . . . marry you . . . then I only want to . . . d-die!"

He put out his arms and drew her close to him.

"You will marry me," he said, "you will behave yourself, and we will spend our money helping a great number of people to be happy."

"That is . . . what Papa did," Malvina said.

"It was all due to him that I went to help the Maharajah, and discovered his Diamond Mine."

"Oh, Shelton, this is just like a . . . Fairy Story . . . and now . . . because you will marry me . . . it has a happy ending!"

"A very happy ending!" Lord Flore said firmly. "At the same time, you *will* behave yourself, or I will be as extremely angry as I was yesterday!"

"I have . . . said I am . . . s-sorry," Malvina

replied in a soft, hesitating little voice.

He drew her closer.

He did not speak, and she looked up at him a little anxiously.

"I have said I will be . . . exactly the sort of . . . wife you want. You have tamed the 'Tigress.' "

"I very much doubt if that is possible," Lord Flore said, "but at last I can control her."

"How will . . . you do . . . that?" Malvina asked a little nervously.

"With love!" Lord Flore replied. "A love, my darling, which makes me know I cannot live without you, and however naughty you are, I find you irresistible!"

"Oh, Shelton, that is the most . . . wonderful thing you have . . . ever said to me!" Malvina cried.

"I intend to say a great many more," Lord Flore said. "I cannot tell you, my precious, what a torture it has been ever since I have known you not to tell you how beautiful you are, and how much I adore you!"

"Do you . . . mean," Malvina asked, "that you have . . . loved me . . . for a long time?"

"Ever since I first set eyes on you," Lord Flore replied, "but I knew I had nothing to offer you, and I had no intention of having a wife who was richer than I was!"

"But . . . you did . . . mean to marry me?" Malvina asked. "You said so just now before the Indian arrived."

"How could I let your father's daughter make

such a mess of her life?" Lord Flore replied. "You get into enough trouble when I am there! Heaven knows what it would be like if I were not!"

"There will be no more trouble now that you love me," Malvina said. "And darling . . . darling Shelton . . . all I want to do is to make you happy . . . and for you to think I am . . . wonderful!"

She rested her cheek against his sleeve for a moment. Then she exclaimed:

"Shelton, I have thought of a marvellous idea!"

"What is it?" he asked.

"We can let David and Rosette live in my house, anyhow, for as long as they have nowhere else to go, while I move into the Priory. And please . . . can it be very quickly?"

"Very quickly, as far as I am concerned," Lord Flore replied. "I want you, my darling, I want you with me every minute of the day and night."

"To make sure I am not doing anything . . . foolish or wrong?" Malvina asked provocatively.

"No, so that I can tell you how much I love you, and make sure you love me," Lord Flore replied.

Unexpectedly, he pushed her away from him and stood looking at her.

"What is . . . it?" Malvina asked. "Why are you . . . looking at me like . . . that?"

"How many men have kissed you?" Lord Flore asked.

Malvina stared at him in astonishment.

"No one has kissed me . . . except . . . you."

There was a light in Lord Flore's eyes. But he said very quickly:

"I want you to kiss me."

Malvina moved quickly towards him, but he did not put his arms around her.

She looked up at him, her lips ready for his.

"I am waiting," he said. "You promised to obey me."

"But I —" she hesitated.

He did not move and hurriedly, the colour rising in her cheeks, she pressed her lips lightly against his.

Then his arms enfolded her.

"My darling, my sweet, my precious little love! Now I know you are telling me the truth!"

"How could you . . . think . . . oh, Shelton, you are . . . making me . . . shy!"

"I adore you when you are shy!"

Lord Flore's voice was very deep, and he looked down at her with an expression in his eyes which no woman had ever seen before.

"Heiress or Tigress," he said, "the only thing that matters is that you will be mine — my wife!"

"That is . . . all I . . . want," Malvina answered.

Then he was kissing her, and they were flying in the sky.

There were no troubles, no difficulties, no evil, but only love, and a dazzling light which came from their hearts.

The employees of G.K. Hall hope you have enjoyed this Large Print book. All our Large Print titles are designed for easy reading, and all our books are made to last. Other G.K. Hall books are available at your library, through selected book-stores, or directly from us.

For information about titles, please call:

(800) 223-1244
(800) 223-6121

To share your comments, please write:

Publisher
G.K. Hall & Co.
P.O. Box 159
Thorndike, ME 04986